WHAT ( NECESS... N

The continuing occurrences of missing rocket ships had scientists Earl Norton and Bob Hart confounded. Rockets were successfully being launched into the heavens, they just never came back. The entire situation was shrouded in mystery, leaving Earth scientists scratching their heads in puzzlement. There were many theories flying around. Some said the rockets had simply disappeared into space and were still hurtling endlessly through the void, while others surmised a more ominous fate—abduction by unknown alien forces. But regardless of theories, the rockets had to be found. So Bob Hart and Earl Norton nervously took to the skies in their own ship, determined to solve the riddle of the missing spacecraft. But would they find a simple scientific explanation, or fall into something far more sinister, as they traveled well beyond the stratosphere...

FOR A SECOND COMPLETE NOVEL, TURN TO PAGE 113

Author Portrait

WILLIAM LEMKIN, Ph. D.

Willam Lemkin, 1897-1978

BEYOND THE STRATOSPHERE

By
WILLIAM LEMKIN, Ph. D.

ARMCHAIR FICTION
PO Box 4369, Medford, Oregon 97504

The original text of this novel was first published by Teck Publication, Inc.

Illustrations by Leo Morey

For more information about Armchair Books and products, visit our website at…

www.armchairfiction.com

Or email us at…

armchairfiction@yahoo.com

BEYOND THE STRATOSPHERE

"ANOTHER rocket has disappeared," remarked Bob Hart dryly as he entered. He flung his leather cap in a corner, helped himself to a cigarette from the pocket of my service jacket hanging nearby, and sank into a chair.

"Just vanished...vamoosed...swallowed up," he elucidated between puffs.

"Which makes the sixth rocket in less than two weeks, doesn't it?" I remarked thoughtfully.

"Six is right, Earl," was the reply, "and this last ship was the prize one of the whole lot. We...the boys over at the shops and myself...worked like Trojans on her for the better part of a week. And she cost good old Stratosphere Transport, Inc., a pretty penny to build and equip with all those gadgets and thing-a-ma-bobs and doodads required for this test flight."

"And now she's gone the way the other five have," I said with a slightly bitter laugh. "If Stratosphere Transport, Inc., persists in lavishing thousands of dollars on these darn fool experiments—these *super-altitude* test flights—it's likely to find itself on the rocks...and among others, there's going to be a cracker jack rocket mechanic called Bob Hart out of a job..."

"Not to mention," interjected Bob merrily, "a certain, highly competent stratosphere pilot by the name of Earl Norton."

A few chuckles, and then we grow serious again.

"What's the dope about the latest disappearance, Bob?" I asked.

"Very little different from the other five. The rocket was shot off in just the same way that the rest were dispatched. It was equipped with the very latest in altitude recorders, maximum and minimum thermometers, and compartments for samples of atmosphere, instruments for measuring cosmic rays, ultra-violet rays, infrared rays, and what not."

"And the parachute equipment, of course?"

"Naturally...but we might just as well have kept that down here on Earth, for all the good it did."

"No traces of any return, eh?"

"None whatsoever, Earl. We sent her off as neatly and beautifully as you please, and that's the last anybody has ever seen of her. The company had watchers scattered over a large area of the surrounding country as well as out at sea. There must have been two hundred individual observers detailed to watch for the rocket when she came down—more than four times the number employed for any of the previous altitude rockets. Not to mention the thousands of unofficial lookouts eager to spot the returning projectile, but not a single word of news from any of them."

"What about the fuel?"

"She carried enough *benzite* and liquid oxygen to bring her to an altitude of well over a hundred miles."

"And the other live test rockets? What of their fuel?"

"Sufficient for about the same altitude—that is, from our calculations, which may or may not be all wrong. Hang it all, Earl, that's where the whole mystery lies! We've sent any number of test rockets aloft since the research department of Stratosphere Transport initiated this series of super-altitude experiments. They've all returned to Earth with recorded elevations of 70, 80, 100, 115 miles. Everything was going smoothly—no hitch in our tests—and then we increased the range—and presto! The rockets never come back!"

"They couldn't possibly have left the Earth's gravitational attractions and become wanderers in space, could they Bob?"

"Ridiculous, Earl...and you know it! In order for those projectiles to break away from the Earth's pull, they need a speed of nearly *seven miles per second.* And so far we haven't been able to make a rocket big enough and strong enough to hold the necessary fuel for attaining such a speed."

"Maybe they encountered meteors at that great height and were destroyed?"

"It doesn't seem likely that all of them should have collided with meteors. If it were only a matter of one lone rocket disappearing, then I'd say meteors. But *six* of them? Not a chance, Earl. And even granting the impossible—even though they were smashed by striking a mass of flying matter at that altitude, wouldn't you expect that there would be some sort of wreckage falling back to Earth? But not a piece of any of them has returned—*not a splinter!*"

"By thunder, Bob, it's got *me!*"

"Me too, Earl, and all of us over at the rocket shops as well. The department chief is all het up about it, and the Big Boss himself must be losing plenty of sleep over the entire business."

"Mystery or no mystery, Bob, I think the company ought to quit wasting time and money on these stunts. The primary job on our hands is just what our name stands for—*stratosphere transport.* The company engineers have perfected upper altitude point-to-point rocket flight so that it has become foolproof and dependable. New York to Chicago in an hour—to Los Angeles in less than three hours—to Paris, Moscow, Buenos Aires at a thousand-mile-an-hour speed through the upper atmosphere. Stratosphere Transport, Inc., has a monopoly of stratosphere transportation, and should bend all its efforts to improving its physical equipment, to perfecting its service, to developing methods and devices that would aim to make stratosphere flight even more fool-proof and more reliable than it is now—if that is at all possible—instead of poking away at unattainable altitudes and fantastic dreams of interplanetary conquest."

"Bravo, Earl! A very pretty speech. Bravo again! Maybe you can convince the research department of Stratosphere Transport saying that they're all washed up on this high altitude business...and then again, maybe you can't."

"Of course, Bob, I'm only a pilot, and not a scientist or a research engineer and so my argument probably won't cut much ice. But I still think that all these expensive experiments are a huge waste, no matter which way you look at them. Any high school kid can tell you that spaceflight and interplanetary travel, with our present materials and equipment, is just a myth—that it will remain such until we discover a radically new building material for our rockets and a fuel that is five times as powerful as the *benzite*-oxygen mixtures now in use."

We lapsed into silence for a few moments, interrupted only by a steady drumming, as Bob beat a thoughtful tattoo with his Anger tips on the arm of his chair. Clouds of cigarette smoke trailed lazily upward. Each of us was engrossed in his own musings.

Bob broke the silence. There was eagerness in his voice and tenseness in his manner as he leaned toward me.

"Those six rockets were sent aloft, weren't they? They didn't come back, did they? They didn't hit a meteor or something and crack up, did they? They couldn't have escaped from the Earth's attraction and sailed off into space, could they? Then what's the only remaining possibility?"

"Why...you don't mean that those six rockets are still...why, Bob you're...!"

"No, I'm not crazy Earl...and you've guessed my theory. *Those rockets are still up there!* My opinion is that they have encountered some kind of obstruction at those altitudes..."

"And very probably been smashed to smithereens by the encounter, eh? Pshaw! Absurd...!"

"...or else they have entered the zone of some mysterious force or ray that has stopped their flight and holds them suspended between Earth and sky!"

"What a theory. And now you're going to tell me that the only way to get them back is to sail up there, unhook them from whatever force is detaining them, and tow them all back to Earth..."

"You've guessed it, old man! That's my notion to the letter. The only way we'll ever know what's become of the missing ships is to go up there and look for them—and, it's dollars to doughnuts, we'll And 'em just where they got tangled up in this paralyzing force."

"Doesn't that mean sending a manned rocket-ship up to an altitude at least three times as high as ever attained by a human being?"

"Yes...and what of it? We have the equipment, we have the necessary fuel. We've sent any number of test rockets to nearly that altitude, and they have returned safely. I'm sure it can be done—and I for one would like to be a member of the crew that takes that rocket up."

"And *I*, for *another,* wouldn't care for any such trip. When it comes to gallivanting about through the stratosphere, why, I feel perfectly at home. But as for the wide open spaces beyond...not for this comparatively earthbound mortal!"

Bob jumped up from his seat and grabbed his greasy cap from the corner where he had flung it.

"I still think this idea of mine is a swell one," he blurted, as he made a dash for the door, "and I'm going to see it through, if I don't do another thing in my life."

"Where to in such a terrible hurry?" I inquired in amusement.

"To see the Big Chief himself," he fired back, "and spill this grand idea of mine."

With his head poking back grotesquely through the doorway, he launched his final shot:

"I may be back before long...with an *invitation!* And maybe you'll change your mind!"

SURE enough, Bob Hart came trooping into my room early the next morning, in high glee.

"We're taking No. 43!" he exploded.

"Who is taking No. 43 where?" I inquired sharply.

"Why, Earl, you don't mean to tell me that you've forgotten all about it already?"

"No, I haven't forgotten all about it, but—what have you got up your sleeve now?"

"Well, I went to see the Big Chief as I said I would. Say Earl, that fellow's a brick, if ever there was one. Probably doesn't know me from any of the other mechanics over at the shop, but he listened to everything I had to say. And, would you believe it, Earl, in less than half an hour I had him all worked up over the idea. Called in a couple of his right-hand men, and had me go over the whole thing once more. We had a real powwow together—and now it's all fixed for tomorrow."

"So they agreed to this lunatic flight of yours?"

"You bet they did. They've given me No. 43 for the trip. The boys are going over her right now, installing extra fuel tanks, and checking up on the controls. Of course, there will have to be a pilot along—I'm only a rocket mechanic—a pretty rotten one at that—and—well, Earl—they've got it all arranged..."

"What are you driving at?"

"They—that is—Dick Evans is taking out the 2:13 ship for Seattle this afternoon instead of you... You see, Earl, this trip beyond the stratosphere will need an expert pilot and...well, I did happen to mention your name...and the Big Chief, that is..."

"Well, I'll be!"

NOW just what could a fellow do?

Here was Bob Hart as enthusiastic as a schoolboy over his scheme. He was simply obsessed with this idea of his—of shooting off into uncharted space at the limits of the Earth's atmosphere in a mad hunt for some missing rocketships that he firmly believed were being detained by a certain unfathomable force. He had even succeeded in gaining a friendly ear from the high moguls of Stratosphere Transport. Bob was tingling with glee at the prospect of a vast adventure, and he wanted none but myself as his companion—in fact, had arranged it all for me, before I had anything but the faintest intimation as to what he was up to.

Now what could a fellow do? The spark of adventure, though burning only faintly in my make-up, was not totally extinct. I gladdened Bob's heart with the "Yes" for which he was waiting. We plunged feverishly into the details of preparation for this unprecedented journey.

No. 43 was a small sturdily constructed ship that had been employed for several months in experimental flights and in mapping new routes through the stratosphere. Small in structure, but exceptionally fast, it was the ideal vessel for our trip.

Bob and his fellow workers of the rocket shops busied themselves with the necessary alterations in the interior of the ship, while I did what I could in checking the controls and seeing that the various devices were in proper working order. For this was no ordinary flight. I had piloted rocketships on most of the difficult stratosphere routes radiating from our main terminal in New York, and I was reasonably expert in the duties involved. But this trip was to be one never attempted before by man, in any sort of vehicle. Yet, such was the vitalizing contagion of my friend's enthusiasm, that, before long, I was almost as rabidly fervent about this mad scheme as I had at first been coldly indifferent.

"Well, Earl, there she is," remarked Bob proudly late that evening. We were viewing the product of the toil of a score of men working all through the day on No. 43. "She's all set! Fuel enough to lift us 175 miles above the surface of the Earth—space suits for both of us and one to spare—oxygen helmets and enough of the generating chemicals for two weeks' constant supply—a month's rations—individual radio packs—the ship's radio in perfect shape—tools and equipment to meet any emergency."

"All set...even to guns and ammunition, I see," I observed significantly.

"Can't venture out without something along that line too," was his grim rejoinder. "Never can tell what unexpected things we might encounter up there."

How strangely prophetic was this terse statement of Bob's, in the light of later development.

"We're off!"

An ominous hissing of exhaust gases and No. 43, her nose pointing upward at an angle of almost 90 degrees, left the greased ways of the launching frame and pierced the air with ever-gaining velocity. The early morning sun peeped through the port window of our rocket.

We ascended slowly at first, in order to avoid excessive heating while passing through the denser strata of the air, then picked up speed as we emerged into the rarer atmosphere. Seated at the controls, I applied the normal technique of stratosphere flight in the first few minutes of our journey. When the altimeter told us that we were close to ten miles above the Earth's surface, I departed from the usual procedure. Instead of leveling off, as I had done so often before, I put the nose of the ship up into a practically vertical climb. I looked grimly at Bob, hovering at my elbow. He returned a mute glance that was full of meaning. The rocket exhausts, to my ears, seemed to hiss a chorus of defiance to the world below. We were plunging upward into a region that only a few of the hardiest souls had ever dared to penetrate. For a moment, I was beset by fearful misgivings. I was almost ready to regret our foolhardy plunge into the comparative unknown. Yet there was Bob by my side, a steely glint of determination in his eye, the eager craving for adventure delineated in the firm setting of his mouth and jaw. My reprehensible wave of timidity vanished. My lot was cast with Bob to the bitter end.

"Gosh, Earl," breathed Bob in my ear, "I've never been up as high as this." He peered down through one of the windows at the hazy mass which represented *terra firma.*

"Twenty-two miles," I read off mechanically from the instrument panel. A fleeting glance at the chronometer on the left, "Just under thirteen minutes—I'll say that's some climbing, eh, Bob?"

My companion was engaged for the moment in scanning the darkening sky through the overhead window. "Nothing to see yet is there?" he mused. "We've still a good piece to go before we reach...whatever we're going to reach."

With the exhaust tubes singing a merry tune behind us, we kept climbing nearly vertically. Our altitude increased at the rate of about two miles each minute. Of course, even with the friction of the air practically eliminated, I could not hope to approach the 16-mile-a-minute speed which was my normal horizontal velocity in stratosphere piloting. We were lifting a considerable load, and our ascent was naturally slow.

Throughout the course of the flight, we were in constant contact by radio with the Stratosphere Transport field below, as well as with private and government radio stations both near and far. Bob's frequent messages about our progress into uncharted space—and they were tersely dramatic messages indeed—were probably being gobbled up by thousands of eager listeners, both official and otherwise, stationed down below.

As we left the denser atmosphere behind, things took on a different aspect in the world outside our space ship. A deepening twilight settled about us, although the sun was clearly visible through the side port.

"Of course you know," I offered by way of explanation, "that daylight is caused by the diffusion or scattering of the sun's rays by the gas particles of our atmosphere. And, since there is no atmosphere up here—or very little—there can be no daylight—or very little."

Bob Hart nodded knowingly, as though to indicate that he was entirely acquainted with this phenomenon and its causes. Both of us could not help but be fascinated by the spectacle of a blazing sun set in a violet sky—a sky that had now begun to burst forth with large and small pinpoints of light as thousands of stars became visible overhead.

The instrument on the panel registered an outside temperature of 145 below zero Fahrenheit. Within the rocketship it was comfortably warm, thanks to the double-walled construction of the vessel, as well as to our auxiliary heating apparatus that had been in operation since early in the flight.

There was very little in the way of conversation attempted. Each of us was busy with our particular tasks in connection with the propulsion and maneuvering of the space flyer. Once, Bob turned to me with a twinkle in his eye. "Scared?" he asked simply. "I mean, of what's ahead of us."

"Not on your life!" was my prompt retort. Whatever my skepticism might have been yesterday (was it really only yesterday? why it seemed like ages ago)—whatever my hesitancy might have been then, I was honestly commencing to enjoy this mad escapade.

"And you?" I queried in kind.

"Who, *me?*" replied Bob with feeling. "Why, dammit all...I wouldn't want to be anywhere else, except right in No. 43, for all the money in the world!"

And I believe that he honestly meant it.

Forty-eight miles...

The sun sent its blazing rays through the *vitro-quartz* windows of the ship, the intense heat being evident even through this highly insulating material. It was apparent that the almost total absence of air about us removed that shielding effect that so thoroughly tempered the sun's heat down at the Earth's surface. The patches of sky visible through the other windows were now no more than squares of dark velvet studded with jewels of surpassing brilliance.

Ninety-three miles...

"Nothing wrong up at this altitude—apparently," breathed Bob. "The earlier test rockets made this distance with ease—and reported back safely in every case."

We plunged relentlessly onward. The angle of our flight was still almost 90°. The vertical mileage clicked off steadily. The ominous tension increased. We were plunging furiously ever upward into the limitless emptiness of space. We might just as well be half-way to the moon for the appearance of things. And we know that we were fast entering that mysterious region of the missing rocket vehicles. At least, I knew that Bob was thinking of nothing else. And, as for me...why...dash it all! I was prepared to admit that I had actually begun to accept the same scatterbrain notion that my giddy friend entertained. Yes...this was the area that held the nefarious secret of the six lost space vehicles. And it was up to us to solve the dark mystery. That was our mission...

Our plan of campaign was of necessity very sketchy. Since we had started forth with no conception of what we were going to encounter, we couldn't have prepared any very systematic scheme of action.

"We ought to level off soon," suggested Bob—"let's stay at about 130 miles. We can scout around at this elevation for a spell—and then shoot up higher if necessary."

I fell in with the plan. Bob had been at the control levers operating the battery of searchlights that enabled the exploration of space in any desired direction. He bent to his task anew, his face pressed against the *vitro-quartz* window, eagerly scanning the emptiness outside.

"Well, here goes!" I remarked gaily. "One-hundred and thirty-three. I'll swing her down gradually and…"

A terrific jolt sent a quiver through the ship. A peculiar sound, half-grinding, and half-sloshing, filled my ears; as though No. 43 were ripping through a mixture of gravel and soft cheese. The sharp impact flung me violently against the control panel. I held on grimly to the corner of the instrument board, while my feet steadied themselves automatically against the floor of the chamber. I was dazed no less by the suddenness of the whole thing than by its violence.

The collision, or whatever it was, had apparently put our illuminating system out of kilter, and only a single emergency bulb glowed feebly over the control board. I could see Bob curled up in a heap in the corner where the first jolt had precipitated him. He did not move.

With a half-cry in my throat, I stumbled blindly along the wall toward the spot where his grotesquely crumpled form lay. The going was precarious. Our ship was still lunging crazily, her speed apparently diminished little. Straining and creaking in every member and at every joint of her sturdily constructed body. No. 43 was ripping along toward seemingly inevitable destruction.

Hours seemed to have elapsed since the first shock, although it was a matter of only a few seconds. I had traversed about half of the distance to my unconscious companion. Suddenly the ship was flung sharply on her side. My uncertain grasp on whatever object I happened to be holding on to at the moment was entirely insufficient to save me from calamity. My fingers were torn violently from their grip and I felt myself being hurled bodily through space. For a fleeting instant I visioned a kaleidoscopic smear of lights and colors. Then my head struck something hard with a resounding smack. My senses abruptly departed.

MY first impression when I came to was the curious absence of motion and sound. I opened my eyes. The surroundings were familiar, although the angle of things was not quite the usual one. In my befuddled condition, it took me an appreciable time to conclude that the rocket vessel must be lying on its side.

"Hello, old man!" came a cheery voice, and I first became aware of Bob Hart bending over me. A funny looking white cloth was about his head and cocked over one ear. I was about to laugh at his ludicrous aspect, and then I was minded to bring my hand to my own head, which had suddenly begun to make its presence vividly real by a sharp jab of pain. I touched the folds of a crudely arranged bandage across my forehead.

"By thunder! What's happened?" I mumbled as I sat up and gazed around at the scene of confusion about the room.

"Hanged if I know," vouchsafed Bob simply. "We must have hit something big and solid—no question about that."

"A meteor?" I ventured.

"Maybe," Bob replied, "although I was watching pretty carefully at the moment we struck—and there was nothing in sight overhead—I'm absolutely certain about that!"

"You had your lights playing directly in our path?"

"All the time, and not a doggone thing in sight—and suddenly *plunk!*—we run right into it—and I get knocked cold."

"Yes, and then it was my turn to bump my head against something hard and unyielding."

"After which I come to and find you stretched out here like a flounder—and it took me the good part of an hour to bring you around."

"Thanks, old fellow, but," and I looked around anxiously, "the ship's not moving! We've landed *somewhere!*"

"If that was a meteor we hit," suggested Bob, "then we must have turned right around and fallen all the way back to where we came from."

"What!" I interposed heatedly. "A hundred and thirty odd miles of free fall! Don't be ridiculous, Bob.

There wouldn't be enough left, either of us or of No. 43, to sweep up into a dustpan."

"Well, then, we must be on another planet," mused Bob, "or maybe a comet or some bit of flying matter that has trapped us and is carrying us out into space."

"Have you had a look outside?" I asked, at the same time reaching up painfully to get to the window over my head.

"Yes, and I can't make it out at all," was the puzzled reply.

Together we stood up and gazed out. The sky presented that same velvet black appearance, with millions of brighter and dimmer specks of light sprinkled over its wide expanse. Our ship was half-over on its side, and resting on some kind of dark and totally unfamiliar surface. The landscape too was decidedly, very odd. We were lying on a slight rise of ground, which stretched down and away from us in a series of gentle depressions and elevations. A glance through the opposite windows revealed the same undulating surface receding from our position.

"This certainly isn't the Earth," I ventured.

"And it can't be Mars, or the moon, or a star or something," added my friend.

The only way to solve the mystery, we soon agreed, was to step out and do some exploring. Very likely, we opined, this enigmatic incident was in some way tied up with the fate of the missing rocketships.

We struggled into our space suits, albeit with considerable difficulty, because of the recently acquired aches and pains in various portions of our anatomy. Constructed of the newly developed *tungstone* fiber, these suits provided for their wearers a uniformly normal pressure on the surface of the body under all sorts of the extreme conditions obtaining without—whether it was the excessive pressures encountered in deep sea diving, or the complete absence of pressure found in a total vacuum. We discarded the crude swathing of bandages that Bob had improvised for both of us. What were a few assorted lacerations and contusions in the sudden thrill of our new adventure? And furthermore, the cloth wrappings interfered seriously with our oxygen helmets—in fact, made it entirely impossible even to get them on. So the surgical paraphernalia went by the board. With our helmets in place, we took a moment or two to see that the compact radio converser in each was in perfect order.

"Okay, Earl," came Bob's cheery voice through the earpieces, after an exchange of messages. "All set to go!"

"Don't forget your gun," I remarked significantly, as I reached for my own and stowed it away in the pocket of my space suit.

The double air lock of the rocket chamber gave us no little difficulty. The rough handling which our ship had undergone had jammed something in the mechanism, and it required considerable exertion to pry open the second of the two airtight flaps. Finally, we mastered the balky locks, and, stepping up and out of our semi-supine ship, we clambered down to solid ground.

No, it was not very solid, we soon found out. "Feels like sponge rubber, doesn't it?" commented Bob. My foot sank several inches into the soft surface and rebounded as I shifted my weight to the other foot.

"And say, Earl, isn't it beastly cold out here?" complained my friend. I nodded in agreement. The intense cold penetrated even the nearly perfect insulation of our *tungstone* suits. I glanced at the temperature-recording instrument built like a wristwatch on the left sleeve of my space garment.

"No wonder," I remarked. "Look at what the thermometer has to say: 256° below zero Fahrenheit! And while we're at it, how about the pressure?" I consulted the instrument on my right wrist. "Zero millimeters of mercury—no air—an *absolute vacuum!*"

Our attention reverted to the curiously spongy ground. It appeared to be composed of flat slabs of material, varying widely in size and shape, and arranged in strata and overlapping layers, like shingles on a roof. Some slabs were uniformly and evenly placed. Others were scattered about with no apparent system. In the immediate vicinity of our rocketship, the surface of the ground seemed to be more than ordinarily disturbed. The slab strata were buckled up in wrinkles of folds, as though showing the result of a great upheaval. Curiously enough, we observed, none of the individual sponge plates were dislodged from position. The corrugations of the ground were not of single slabs, but of whole layers of them. Truly, I could remember nothing on Earth that resembled this peculiar construction.

From an examination of the puzzling nature of the ground beneath our feet, we turned to an exploration of what could be seen overhead. Bob uttered an exclamation and pointed aloft.

"I'll be darned, Earl! Isn't that the moon?"

"Sure it's the moon, and nothing else!"

There was no denying it. That silvery satellite of ours was too familiar a sight to be mistaken for anything else. There she hung, low in the sky off to our left, her craters and mountains and valleys forming that combination of light and shadow that constituted the familiar face of the "Man in the Moon."

And then my eyes roamed over the expanse of jeweled sky above us. I was no adept at astronomy, but I had little trouble in identifying several familiar constellations. I called Bob's attention to them and he verified my observations.

We marveled at the curious combination of things which assailed our senses in this strange region into which we had been so unceremoniously dumped. Here was an absolutely unprecedented confusion of various phenomena—some commonplace, some unusual—some ordinary, some bizarre. Was this the Earth? Was this some other planet or heavenly body in space? Where in thunder were we?

BOB and I were in no position to determine our situation adequately. We had not yet seen enough of the place to form any definite conclusions. We must explore further. Perhaps we would soon come to an adequate explanation of our strange predicament.

Scrambling down the slope from the elevated point where the ship had come to rest, we continued our reconnoitering expedition. The going was very easy, what with the curiously springy nature of the ground as well as the seemingly diminished gravitational effect.

"I wonder," remarked my companion, "if we'll find any kind of living creatures out here in this God-forsaken country."

"I can't see how any form of life could possibly maintain itself here," I replied. "The conditions aren't exactly what you'd call ideal. However, let's be on the lookout."

It soon became apparent to us that there was nothing in the immediate vicinity of our ship to give us much information as to our whereabouts. We must extend our area of exploration. However, of necessity, we must not lose contact with the ship itself. Neither of us could venture even a guess as to the possible dangers that might befall us in this bizarre land of sponginess and semi-darkness. And good old No. 43, partly disabled though she was, represented our only link with the world from which we had come (wherever that might be right now).

We took careful note of the position of the ship with relation to certain of the more easily distinguishable landmarks. We also made some approximation at compass directions by observation of the stars. Wherever or whatever this land might turn out to be, at least we could safely plot our journeyings by the location of the well-known star groupings overhead. We were thankful for that fortunate circumstance.

The way to the west appeared to be mostly downhill and less ragged in its topography than any other. We therefore took that direction. The choice was a lucky one, as brought out by subsequent developments.

The way led down a gradual slope into a sort of ravine. This wound off to the northwest for a short distance, and then led out upon another stretch of flat land. Following that open area we crossed a slight ridge, then dipped once more into the gully that turned west again. Here and there we observed a stunted form of vegetation in the shape of a low scraggy bush, growing to a height of about a foot or less. Perhaps this was the only form of organic matter in this unusual domain, for we could observe no evidence of insect or other animal life. And as for intelligent living beings…

About a half hour of tramping in a generally westerly direction added very little to our existing fund of information about this curious land.

"Let's go back to the ship," I suggested, "and start off on another track. Maybe we picked the worst direction at the very start."

Bob readily agreed that there was no point in following our present angle of attack any longer. We were about to retrace our steps, when Bob seized me by the arm and pointed to the left of our position.

"See that haze?" he breathed.

I followed his gesture. A slight ridge ran east and west several hundred feet from our present location. The brow of this elevation was strangely lit up as by a pink halo. It appeared to denote some kind of illumination on the other side—not a steady illumination, but one that flickered mysteriously.

"I'd say it's a bonfire," suggested Bob.

"A bonfire…in a vacuum? Nonsense!" I replied.

"Let's see what it is," he ventured.

We made our way cautiously up the slight rise toward the crown. The pink glow seemed to grow stronger, and the flickering more pronounced. Crawling on our stomachs, we slowly approached the crest of the ridge. We attained the summit and peered anxiously over.

The sight that met our astonished eyes was one not easily erased from our memory.

In the centre of the wide depression lay the missing rocketships…

Five of them were lying side by side on the ground, as though lined up for inspection. The sixth, which I immediately recognized from its size and general appearance as the latest of the vessels to have disappeared into space, lay by itself somewhat off to the side.

But the thing that nearly took our breath away was the bewildering maze of pink lights about the rocket projectiles. Small, glowing spots of pink light—and they twisted and squirmed and meandered all around and over the ships.

"Look!" breathed my companion tensely. "They're some kind of living things!"

Sure enough, when my eyes had become accustomed to the eerie glow, I could make out dim shadowy forms that moved about. Apparently, the glowing knobs of pink light were attached to these moving beings. And what grotesque beings…

They were roughly cubical in shape, and about two feet in height, with innumerable hair-like projections or tentacles that extended out from the body in all directions. The organism was made of some semi-transparent material resembling gelatine, which quivered and flowed with every motion of the body. From the top surface of the cube there grew out two longer and thicker tentacles, each terminating in a rounded knob. And it was this knob that threw forth that ghostly pink glow.

There were hundreds—perhaps *thousands*—of these extraordinary beings, all of them moving about in feverish haste around and over the assembled rocketships. It was very evident to us both, as we crouched apprehensively on the rim of the hollow, that they were engaged in some exceedingly hectic activity. As the cubical organism swarmed over the ships their translucent bodies quivered and their hair-like tentacles lashed and squirmed in a most uncanny fashion. But most stupendous of all to our bewildered eyes

The sixth, which I immediately recognized from its size and general appearance as the latest of the vessels to have disappeared into space, lay by itself somewhat off to the side.

was the swaying and bobbing of the glowing bulbs at the extremities of the thicker appendages.

For the space of several minutes, Bob and I watched this unearthly spectacle in speechless amazement. Then my companion broke the silence with a hoarsely whispered question.

"What do you make of it, Earl?"

"We've found the missing rockets all right, Bob—and plenty more too!"

"Those bugs—or whatever the creatures may be—certainly are flocking all over the ships like a swarm of flies around an overturned jug of molasses."

"By George...do you see what I see? Why those rockets...*they're half dismantled!*"

"Gosh, Earl, you're right! Those blooming bugs have nearly picked the ships apart. Let's move up closer and get a better look."

We crawled a few feet nearer to the extraordinary scene of activity, and confirmed this startling observation. The five projectiles lying in the group together were literally mere shells of their former selves. Various surface plates had been removed, to reveal the vitals of the rocket mechanisms. Parts of the machinery could be seen lying about on the ground. Firing chambers, expulsion tubes, portions of the balancing fins, extra fuel containers...it was evident that the rocketships had been pretty thoroughly dissected.

"And they're still at it...those bugs!" I breathed into my mouthpiece.

The swarming jelly-cubes were engaged in the task of tearing the space vessels apart—yet there was methodicalness and system about the entire uncanny procedure. This was no mere act of vandalism or wanton destruction...

THESE beings were occupied in a careful and exhaustive study of the captured vessels—for that was really what the rocketships were. As we watched the doings below in openmouthed and open-eyed astonishment, we could see a half-dozen organisms manipulating a hinged panel from one of the air locks. Bulky and heavy though it was, they lifted it from its fastenings with ease, and bore it over the side of the vessel. Gently they deposited it on the ground alongside of several more panels that had doubtlessly been removed from the other ships with equal facility and dispatch. Following this operation, the beings hastened back to proceed with the task of dismemberment. Similar scenes were taking place over the entire area of activity. The whole performance reminded me strongly of the bustle and haste that is observed about a good-sized anthill.

"Look at how they lift things!" whispered Bob. "They use those funny-looking horns with the pink headlights."

It was obvious that these cubical beings possessed enormous physical power which was concentrated in the knob-like antennae. There was no clutching or holding the heavy parts of the rocketships as each portion was removed. Instead the creatures applied the glowing bulbs to the surface of the object and then lifted the mass as though it were weightless.

And not only were these magical appendages employed for lifting and carrying. My companion called my attention to a spot off to the side where one of the rocket tool kits had been deposited. There a group of cube beings were tackling the metal box, the cover of which had become jammed, probably as a result of the impact landing. Evidently failing to disengage the locking mechanism, they were attacking the cover with their shining knobs. Several hel4-the box while one being ran the glowing tips of his antennae appendages along the edge of the cover. Two faintly luminous streaks appeared in the wake of the moving bulbs. The metal seemed to be sheared as though by an oxy-acetylene torch of needlelike thinness. In a few moments the recalcitrant cover was completely severed, and fell away at the mere touch from the all-powerful knob of another of the cube beings.

More startling, almost, than anything else was the disintegrating power of these appendages. In slicing through the solid matter of the rocket structure the mysterious ray or other emanation from the luminous knob simply reduced the substance attacked into nothingness. The stuff was just melted away as if by a powerful flame. The effect was truly supernatural.

"They've got power in those headlight horns!" commented Bob in an awed whisper.

"They could do almost anything with them," I agreed.

"Anything!" echoed my companion. "Look over there, Earl. Do you see that group standing off to the side as though watching the show? And there are other clusters of idlers all about. You can see them bunched together waving their extension lights at each other and at the rest of the fellows who are working on the rocketships. Those pink knobs must also be some kind of device for communication. Either they are transmitting messages and orders to the ones that are doing the dismantling job, or else they are carrying on a sort of conversation with each other."

There was no denying that Bob's observation and conclusion were very plausible indeed. From the agitated antennae-waving of the cube creatures standing at the sidelines, so to speak, it was easily discernible that the appendages were also capable of transmitting intelligent thought from being to being.

I do not know how long we lay there and watched this unearthly spectacle. Minutes slipped by—perhaps hours.

The fascination of the phenomenon before us made time stand still.

Presently a change became apparent. The group of creatures nearest to our hiding place stopped the mysterious waving and tossing of glowing pink knobs. The squads of workers engaged in dismembering the ships halted in their tasks. The more distant clusters of cubes gradually abated their frenzied activity. As if by magic, the agitation ceased. A death-like calm engulfed the little valley. Only here and there a single luminous knob waved almost imperceptibly—here and there a feeble pink glow blazed forth with exaggerated brilliance, then died down to faint luminosity once more.

Bob Hart and I exchanged glances of astonishment. What in thunder was the meaning of this abrupt paralysis down there? We peered into the valley again…

Suddenly another change became evident. The group nearest to us—the one that had been first to cease its activities—began to show signs of returning life. Again appendages waved and pink bulbs glowed. But there was an ominous something about the new activity. There was more agitation, more excitement, more suppressed tension apparent.

"Good Lord!" muttered Bob. "Could it be…? Maybe they've discovered our presence, Earl! Maybe…"

The workers on the captive spaceships had not resumed their tasks. Instead, there was a gradual flow of cube beings over the sides of the recumbent vessels. They waddled and squirmed over mechanical parts and the assorted rocket equipment strewn about the scene. They were converging upon the cluster of their fellow creatures that had started the sudden shift of activity. Off to the left and right other groups of the creatures were beginning to stir. All were moving toward one spot—the place directly below our point of concealment.

Could those enigmatic creatures, with their mysterious powers of divination, have become aware of our presence? So far, I had not thought of associating fear or danger with these beings. But now a sudden wave of apprehension engulfed us. Were they hostile? Were they harmless? Should we reveal ourselves? Should we take to our heels?

"Looks like they are wise to us," I whispered. "They're holding some kind of council of war."

"And look at that fellow over there," replied Bob, "—the one with the reddish-pink headlight! He seems to be doing all the talking, judging from the way he swings those bulbs around."

"We'd better be ready to move," I breathed. "If those bugs start coming for us our best bet is to show them our heels. No telling how they'd feel toward us."

"Right!" vouchsafed my friend, grimly. "It's back to No. 43 for us the minute those babies show any real sign that they're on to us."

For a few tense minutes, the swarms of creatures in the valley contented themselves with hobnobbing and powwowing as though discussing a plan of action. All work on the six space vessels was now at a standstill. The vigorous waving of antennae and the swaying and gliding of pink bulbs denoted the equivalent of a heated discussion. Then...

"Here they come! They've spotted us, Earl! *Let's go!*"

As the horde of jelly-cubes came swarming up the incline we leaped to our feet and made off in the direction from which we had so recently come. At least it was the general direction in which we thought our rocketship lay. A fervent prayer was in my heart—that we do not go astray and miss No. 43—and I was positive that my panting friend at my side entertained the same earnest hope.

A glance behind showed that in running prowess we were more than a match for our cubical pursuers. The uncanny sponginess of the surface under our feet and the apparent diminution of gravitational force served to make our progress one succession of enormous leaps and bounds.

But even if we *were* to succeed in reaching the shelter of our rocketship, would we be safe there? Through my mind, as I ran, there flashed the scene of the disemboweled projectiles behind us, with the flocks of cubical beings tearing and cutting the rocket shells as though they were made of cardboard. But why cross bridges…

A FEW minutes of running had widened the lead we had taken over our pursuers, that they were visible as merely a pink glow in the rear. We stopped to take our bearings. Were we heading the right way? There was no telling how much actual distance we had put between ourselves and No. 43 in our trip of exploration. In the dim starlight, it was impossible to see very far in any direction.

"We'll just have to trust to luck," I panted. "If we miss the ship, then…"

By this time, the pursuing mob of creatures had shortened by half the distance between us. The first of the swarm were just emerging over a low ridge behind us, their glowing appendages waving briskly. The ominous pink haze beyond the vanguard indicated that the rest were not far to the rear.

Once more, we were off, scrambling down into a gully and up the other side in the general direction where we thought our ship lay. A few minutes of prodigious running—which was nothing more than a glorified "hop-skip-and-jump" game—brought us well ahead of the cube creatures once more.

And then…

We emerged from a broad shallow valley and up a gentle slope…and there was our rocketship, half over on its side, just as we had left her, I don't know how many hours ago.

Good old 43...no sight could have been more welcome at this precise moment.

Bob and I galloped up the spongy slope and tackled the air-lock panel. Involuntarily a groan escaped my lips. The infernal lock! The mechanism had become jammed in some manner, and could not be budged. I recalled that this self-same device had given us no little trouble on the occasion of our quitting the ship some time ago. And now, at this critical stage, the balky locking gadget refused to operate.

We tugged manfully and swore softly. Confound it! On our way out the blamed lock had worked—after a while—and after a fashion. Certainly, it couldn't go back on us now!

I relinquished my grip on the door handle, and shot a glance over my shoulder. Just as I thought! The vanguard of the cube creatures was in sight. Pink bulbs glowing fiercely, antennae beating about furiously, gelatinous masses waddling grotesquely as they rushed upon us.

In the eerie half-light from the star-speckled dome of the heavens, this advancing horde presented a terrifying spectacle indeed.

With a cry, I whipped out my automatic from its sheath in my space suit and let fly at the wobbling masses that swept toward us. I pumped away as fast as my finger could work the trigger. And now my weapon was empty...and still they came on relentlessly. Good lord...were these hideous creatures immune to flying lead? Apparently so. Surely, I had made some direct hits in that thickly crowded mass of cubical bodies. Yet there was no more impression made than if I had been pelting them with peas. Only the most imperceptible wavering of the ranks, and then they were on their way again toward us with the grim relentlessness of an onrushing flood.

I was momentarily paralyzed by the fearsome sight. Then a sharp cry of exultation from Bob broke the spell. I wheeled swiftly. During my ineffectual bombardment, he had continued his struggle with the obstinate mechanism. And now he had the door open. In a twinkling, he had me by the arm and flung me bodily into the narrow inner compartment of the air lock. Scrambling in behind me, he slammed the door shut again, just as the first of the pursuing creatures hurled themselves upon the ship.

The second hatch leading into the control chamber of the vessel gave us but little difficulty. We tumbled through the opening and lay panting on the floor. We could do no more for the space of several moments.

"Whew! That was a narrow squeak!" gasped Bob. I had not yet caught my breath, so the best I could do was nod weakly in reply.

"What do you say if we get rid of this truck we're carting around," continued my chum. He suited action to words by flinging off his helmet and struggling out of his space suit. I did likewise, and presently we stood facing each other, smiling, and hands gripped, as though greeting one another after a long separation.

"And now about our little friends outside," I remarked. We could plainly detect a soft scraping sound on the outer surface of the ship, above our heads and on all sides.

"That's them!" said Bob, tersely, if ungrammatically. "They're climbing all over us. Look Earl...there at that window!"

I followed his glance. One of the creatures was pressed close to the transparent surface. More joined him. Soon a whole group of them was clustered there. I looked about in dismay. The other windows were now similarly decorated. The cube beings were crowding each other at every port, their glowing blubs waving briskly at us.

We prepared to resist the onslaught—although I was frank to admit to myself that, the means at our command for such resistance was pitifully weak. What about that stream of bullets I had sent in their direction only a few minutes ago?

"Shall we try a getaway?" asked my companion. "We can shake this whole crowd in a jiffy by giving her the gun."

"But where to?" I queried. "We don't know where we are. We may be worse off somewhere else—if we ever manage to get there. How do we know that the bump of landing here didn't put our driving mechanism out of commission? We better hang on here, and see what turns up. So far those fellows haven't started to do us any harm."

"You're right, old man," replied Bob seriously. "If they meant to injure us they would have started their dirty job by now."

"And they certainly could make short work of this old crate, if they wanted to," I added. "You saw how those other ships looked over in that valley, didn't you? Well, what's preventing them from making mincemeat out of No. 43 in three shakes of a pink headlight?"

"And speaking of headlights," said Bob, "just look at the way they're waving those bulbs at the windows. Darned if I don't think they're trying to communicate a message to us—and darned if I could make out what it is they're trying to say."

I soon agreed with my friend that the curious creatures were very evidently not hostile, and that their persistent antennae waving denoted some attempt on their part to communicate with us. The groups of beings remained crowded at the various windows for many minutes, and they kept up the constant swaying of illuminated appendages. The pattering and scraping on the surface of the ship could still be heard. Presently that sound ceased. Soon the groups began to thin out at the windows. One by one, they left their posts and slid out of sight. And now they were all gone—each transparent panel revealed only a patch of star-sprinkled sky.

Bob and I looked at each other with apprehension, and edged cautiously to the nearest port. We peered out. The cube men had retreated to a distance of several hundred yards and were massed together there as though holding a council of war. A hasty glance through the other windows revealed that they were congregated in a wide circle about the ship.

WE came back to our original observation post and anxiously watched the developments without. Apparently, all was quiet on the cubical front. The army of creatures maintained their position with no further moves, either hostile or otherwise. We did observe at length that the ranks of our besiegers were beginning to thin out. In small groups, they were departing from the scene of activity. We could see clusters of pink lights moving down the slope stretching away from our position, and disappearing over the edge of the distant ridge. Were they giving up the siege? Were they abandoning their attempt to get us out of our stronghold? Were they cooking up some new campaign, some new strategy? We had no way of knowing. All we could do was guess—and, under the circumstances, I was ready to confess that we were miserably poor guessers.

Minutes dragged along with no sign of any new move on the part of the cubical beings surrounding our ship. The remaining cluster of native creatures kept their distance from us...and did nothing. Bob and I relaxed our extreme tension. My comrade dropped on one of the cots, while I sank into a chair nearby. We fell to discussing our very odd predicament.

We went over all the incidents of our trip from the moment we left the Earth. Everything appeared to have gone normally at the start. Up to an altitude of one hundred and thirty odd miles, our progress had been uneventful. Our minds were vividly clear about each succeeding step up to that point.

"And then...*kerplunk!*" said Bob, with a sweep of his hand toward one of the windows, "...we run right into *this*..."

From the moment of the terrific impact that had knocked us both senseless, our thoughts and sensations were one dizzy confusion. The spongy ground—the absence of atmosphere—the familiar celestial manifestations of moon, stars and constellations. Then the lost rocketships—the gelatinous cube men with their luminous appendages—the mad chase back to our vessel—our present imprisonment, for, whichever way we regarded the matter, we were virtual prisoners.

"But the missing rocketships," repeated Bob, "we found them after all. At least that part of the mystery is cleared up, even though the rest of it is still one grand puzzle."

More discussion and comment back and forth, without reaching any satisfactory explanation of our present plight.

"There's one thing we haven't done yet," I suggested. "When we first tumbled into the ship after that wild chase, you mentioned a possible getaway. I didn't think much of the idea then. But it strikes me that we ought to look into it now. Not exactly for a getaway, mind you. But if we could get the ship off the ground, we could do some exploring around these parts. And we could do it safely—comparatively speaking."

Bob readily fell in with my idea. An examination of our fuel supply revealed that we had on hand slightly less than half the quantity with which we had started the trip. When we came to the driving mechanism, however, we met a situation which each of us in his heart had dreaded, although each of us had, up to this point, been unwilling to put his fears into words. The shock of our precipitous landing in this strange region had seriously damaged our rocket apparatus. We carefully tested each firing chamber and each exhaust tube in turn. Three of the propulsive units behaved beautifully. The other twelve were either lifeless or else hopelessly erratic in their operation; a truly heartbreaking performance.

Bob went over the mechanism carefully. After some extensive tinkering, he was willing to confess that the damage to the balky units was more considerable than could be corrected with the tools and spare parts at present on hand. We eyed each other with dismay.

"We're stuck!" grunted my companion as he threw down a wrench and wiped the beads of perspiration from his brow with the back of his oil-stained glove. "Can't even *think* of budging her on only three units—and I don't know how we'll ever get the others repaired. Unless!" and his face suddenly brightened as a happy thought seemed to flash into his mind.

"Unless what?" I queried sharply.

"Those six prisoner ships over yonder!" he replied tensely. "By George, there are enough parts in those hulks to patch us up in great shape, and to spare. And then there's the fuel...must be plenty left in the tanks. If only we could get over there and lay our hands on the stuff...!"

His voice trailed away into dismal silence. I could see the hopelessness of his wish. Here we were cooped up in our tiny shell like rats in a trap and encircled by that band of jelly-like creatures. The six vessels with their plentiful reserve of precious fuel and that assortment of replacement parts for our damaged machinery might just as well be back on Earth or up there on the moon, for all the good we could get out of them.

Our present thoughts as well as tasks were abruptly terminated by a renewed activity on the part of the cube men. In our preoccupation with the job of examining and testing, we had forgotten them for the time being. And now they were brought back to our attention by a renewal of the familiar scraping and thumping on the outer surface of the ship. At the same time, we could see groups of them clustering at the windows again, crowding each other at every one of the panels.

Instinctively we reached for our automatics. This meant an attack and nothing else—although we realized fully how puny was our defense against these creatures.

"They must have been aroused by our test shots through the rocket tubes," breathed Bob apprehensively. "Maybe they have an idea we're getting ready to start action against them."

Fearfully we waited in the centre of the chamber, our eyes skipping from one window to another. Each had its quota of squirming, jostling masses, tentacles weaving and swaying, luminous bulbs glowing weirdly in ever-changing patterns.

Tense minutes passed, with no evidence of the impending attack. Taut nerves slackened. Apprehension dissolved. Frankly, I was beginning to become accustomed to the freaky behavior of these enigmatic organisms.

"I'll be darned, Earl!" My chum broke the silence precipitously. "Did it ever occur to you that we're just afraid of a *bogey-man?* We seem to have the idea that these creatures are out for our skins. But so far, have they really harmed us any? All they've done is chase us back into the ship. And if they really had any intentions of injuring us, what's stopping them from slicing and dicing No. 43 in the same way that we saw them operating on the other space flyers. That would be the easiest way for them to get at us, wouldn't it Earl? And yet, they are satisfied with standing off at a distance, or crowding around at the windows the way you see them right now."

"Well, Bob, what do you think we ought to do?"

"Do? Well, I'll tell you. I've got half a notion that the bet for us would be to go right outside and talk turkey to those bugs."

"*Talk?* What do you mean by talk?"

"Just what I said...*talk!* Why, can't you see, Earl...those beings are really trying to communicate with us. Just look at them. That peculiar motion of their headlights is probably the only way they have of conversing with each other. And all they're trying to do, no doubt, is to talk to us in the only language they are capable of using. Now isn't that a reasonable assumption?"

I was inclined to agree with my keenly observant companion. What shortsighted idiots we had been—to attribute hostile designs to these apparently peaceable denizens of this extraordinary region.

And so we hastily donned our space suits once more and sallied forth through the still balky air lock into the vacuum without. As we emerged, the last of the cube men were just scrambling down from their perch at the rocketship windows. We stepped out upon the spongy slabs, advanced a few paces, and halted. The creatures remained stationed in a compact semicircle. The only motion was that ubiquitous swinging of pink bulbs.

"Darned if I know how to begin!" Bob's voice sounded faintly in my helmet earpieces.

"Let's try waving to them," I ventured back.

WE must have cut an extremely ludicrous appearance, standing there in our bulky space suits, waving our arms in a manner resembling an old-fashioned Boy Scout novice going through a semaphore drill. But it appeared to elicit the desired result. When we commenced our manual oscillations, the motion of the luminous appendages ceased. After a few minutes of energetic signaling on our part, the others resumed their swaying. It was comical—our waving at them, their waving back at us, neither knowing what the other was trying to say.

At any rate, we established one thing—the cubical beings were definitely not hostile, and were evidently trying to transmit intelligent thought to us. That was something to be thankful for. We breathed more freely…

Still maintaining their signaling motions, they closed in about us with an air about them of disarming friendliness. They came almost to within arm's length of us, and we were better able to observe and study their outlandish structure.

Each cubical being was semitransparent, as we had noted before. The gelatinous mass was not uniform in texture, but presented a bewildering conglomeration of large and small patches or globules of darker and lighter hue.

There was nothing stationary about these patches. They quivered and vibrated as though suspended in semisolid gelatine. But uncanny still, was the fact that most of the areas were colored. The larger ones particularly bore characteristic hues that gave the individual a distinctive chromatic *motif*. Looking about I was surprised to see that no two cubes boasted the same identical pattern. However, nearly alike any pair of individuals might be, there was still an elusive something about their color scheme that seemed to distinguish one from the other without possibility of error. And there were hundreds of them crowded about us,—all different. The effect was truly kaleidoscopic.

Presently the encircling mass of cubes opened up before us, offering a cleared path down the slope. The direction was the same one which we had taken on our recent trip of exploration. The nearest of the assembled creatures waved his tentacles at us, and then indicated the passageway lying ahead. Their request was self-evident. Bob and I exchanged questioning glances.

"It looks like they want us to march," I said.

"Well, no harm I guess," he replied. "Let's go!"

We trudged gallantly down the cleared passageway. The cube creatures waved approvingly—at least it was easy to read satisfaction in their movements and their demeanor. They closed in behind us and waddled along as an escort—a huge mob of strangely shaped, strangely colored and strangely lighted beings forming a seeming guard of honor for us in our march through this most unusual region.

Bob and I exchanged but few remarks and those only perfunctory in nature. We were both beginning to enjoy the novel predicament. With the thought of physical danger removed from our minds, at least for the present, this escapade was developing into a real lark.

Soon I began to recognize familiar landmarks. We were nearing the spot where the lost spaceships were being dissected. And in a very few moments we again came upon the scene. It was still one of concerted activity. Swarms of cube men were busily engaged in the same dismembering task that we had been observing from our hiding place only a short time ago. Either a large number of our former pursuers had returned to their tasks during the period that Bob and I had been under siege in our ship, or else their places had been taken by others when the mass of workers had abandoned their jobs to give chase.

We were now motioned to draw closer. Signals flashed between the leaders of our escorting party and the overseers of the dismantling work. Tentacles waved and pink bulbs glowed. Some of the waving and flashing we surmised to be an exchange of messages among the cube men themselves. Part of it seemed to be directed right at us; As if subjected to an intangible urge. Bob and I descended into the work area among the dismantled rocketships.

"There's only one way I can figure it out," my friend said. "These creatures are just plain curious about us and our means of travel—as curious as we are of them and their unusual country. They are burning to know where we come from, how we got here, what makes these space-flyers operate. They've pretty well dismantled the ships in their efforts to get at the bottom of matters. And now that they've stumbled across us, they want to be shown how the whole thing came about. Now isn't that just the way you and I would react if the circumstances were reversed? Even though these organisms are far from human, they display evidence of almost human mental processes."

Again, I was compelled to admit that Bob had analyzed the situation with rare level-headedness. What explanation could be more in keeping with the facts as we had observed them thus far?

"Well," I replied, "let's see what we can show them. Maybe we can make *something* work in that conglomeration of assorted hardware down below. Come on."

"And, while we're at it," continued Bob as we stumbled across the littered area, "now's our chance to see what we could locate in the way of spare parts to repair No. 43. Remember, Earl, we've somehow got to make that old tin can percolate. We're depending on her to bring us back to Earth safely...someday...somehow..."

The assembled creatures followed our movements with rapt attention. At our approach, all work on the six ships ceased. The crowd made way for us readily. The individual cubical beings almost tumbled over each other to get out of our path so that we could work without any interruption. The utmost respect and deference were displayed—it nearly amounted to downright awe.

Bob made a hasty inspection of the nearest ship. Most of the vitals had been removed and laid out on the ground close by. "All the mechanism is here," he grunted, after a cursory check-up, "and most of it's in fair condition, but it would take hours to reassemble the works."

We went on to the second flyer. The cube men closed in around us eagerly.

I could almost feel the aura of curiosity and expectancy that pervaded the very space all about us. The sensation was decidedly creepy.

"This looks better," said Bob laconically. Most of the parts are still intact. Let's see if we can't patch it up a little—just enough so we can give 'em a little demonstration."

The task was not an easy one, but we soon found that there was an abundance of eager assistance available on a moment's notice. In fact, there was a super-abundance of it. The instant Bob beckoned for help in lifting one of the heavy exhaust nozzles there was a flood of gelatinous beings that all but swamped us. We actually had to shoo them off so that they would not be in our way. It was simply miraculous. Just as deftly as the ships had been dismantled, so deftly were the parts restored in the flyer upon which Bob and I were concentrating.

"I don't know if we can put it all together good as new," remarked Bob as the job progressed rapidly. "Some of the works are pretty well shot to pieces—either by the force of the landing, or else by the dismembering job to which the ship was subjected after she got here. Although," he added contemplatively, "from what we've seen of their work, these cube mechanics have shown remarkable care and even skill in tearing her apart. Well, all we can hope to do is to patch up one or two of the rockets units, and give them a sort of static demonstration."

As the work went on, I soon became aware of something noteworthy. Among the large flock of willing helpers that persisted in tumbling all over us and each other in their eager endeavor to lend their aid, I observed two that displayed even more eagerness than the rest. These two creatures were always at our elbows—lifting, cutting, prying, or hauling. I soon called Bob's attention to them. He had already become cognizant of the situation himself.

"Just look at them, will you!" I observed, "They're simply dying to be of help. Now take that one with the bright red polka dots all throughout his body. He's been slaving like an automatic machine at this job, and doesn't seem to get tired."

"No more peppy than his friend over there, with the pea-green spots," replied Bob. "By George," he added, "*Red* and *Green* are doing more work between them than any given dozen of their countrymen—and goodness knows the rest of them are no slouches by any means."

And so *Red* and *Green* they were forthwith christened. A couple of energetic fellows they proved to be and also endowed with phenomenal strength and stamina. They just clung to us like a couple of faithful hounds, always there to lend a hand—or rather a tentacle—in making a task lighter. And they demonstrated a phenomenal brand of intelligence. They seemed to read our thoughts and anticipate every one of our needs. A remarkable pair…

Well, the job was finally finished—after a fashion. Bob succeeded in patching together two rocket units. We found a fairly considerable amount of spare fuel in the various tanks of the six ships—a fortunate circumstance we agreed between ourselves, for we could make use of it all in our not-so-distant endeavor to get back to Earth.

"We'll have to go easy with this stuff," Bob said earnestly. "Can't go wasting too much of it on spectacular stunts like this one."

WE now waved the multitude of cubes back to a respectable distance, where most of them congregated in obviously eager anticipation of a dramatic demonstration. A few of the leaders stood close by to watch our manipulations. *Red* and *Green* were among this group. Bob adjusted the trigger mechanism for remote control firing, and then we stood back. Frankly, we did not expect anything very startling—and we were not disappointed. The two rocket chambers began firing nearly simultaneously, and continued to discharge for nearly a minute. Bluish-white flames spurted from the exhaust nozzles, scorching the ground for a distance of several feet. The ship, lying there on its side, responded only feebly to the driving impulse. She bucked and quivered for the duration of the firing period, then settled back serenely.

The demonstration was over almost in less time than it takes to tell it, yet it made a remarkable impression on the assembled spectators. The creatures had been tensely motionless during the few moments of the actual test. Now they commenced their everlasting tentacle waving once more; only it was more vigorous and more meaningful than before. This was evidently their form of applause and approval. They crowded about us, with *Red* and *Green* always among the nearest to us. The cube men were pleased. The demonstration had, to them, been a huge success, and they were letting us know that they had liked it immensely.

I recalled that this was really the second demonstration we had given these people. The first one had been on the occasion only a short time ago, when we had tested out the rocket discharges while besieged in our own vessel. I remembered that the cube men had withdrawn to a distance at the time, and the start of our firing tests was the signal which brought the creatures flocking back to our windows in bewilderment and surprise. Only this present spectacle was more in the nature of a planned presentation. And the creatures accepted it as a phenomenal accomplishment. At least that much was evident from their signals of approval and encouragement.

We honestly did not know what we had succeeded in demonstrating to the bizarre inhabitants of this region, but we were certain of one thing, and we did not hesitate to assure ourselves of it and rejoice over it together, even in the confusion that surrounded us for the moment. We had proved to our own satisfaction that there were materials and means available here to make all necessary repairs on our own ship—when the time came—and make her fit to start back with us to civilization—also when the time came.

But now our chief object was to take advantage of the situation in which we found ourselves at present. Undoubtedly, we had gained the respect and admiration of the cubical natives. Our slightest wish was their holy command. It behooved us to capitalize on our unexpected advantages.

While we were receiving the luminous plaudits of the assembled cubical multitude, the sun rose. The phenomenon was of course nothing like a terrestrial sunrise. The flaming orb appeared suddenly above the eastern edge of the valley and shot steadily upward into the indigo sky. The myriads of stars remained unchanged in the dark dome of the heavens, adding their feeble illumination to the eerie yellow glow cast over the scene by the rising sun.

The rocket demonstration being over, the cube men appeared to be highly pleased. They now closed in upon us from three sides leaving a cleared passageway for us. By their gesticulations, they endeavored to convey an invitation. Clearly, they wanted to escort us somewhere else. Again, we trudged along dutifully across spongy plains and over hills and through valleys of resilient rubberlike substance. Somehow, we could not feel any apprehension. There was something totally disarming about the naive, almost childlike simplicity of these creatures. Bob and I conversed in whispers as we tramped along in this curious convoy of waddling jelly cubes and bobbing globes of light. We agreed that it was the grandest lark ever given humans to experience. We were determined to see it through at all cost.

"Say, Earl," remarked Bob presently. "Do you feel as warm as I do?"

"Do I?" was my retort. "It's just sweltering here inside this suit of mine!"

The sun had been advancing steadily as we marched, and was now beating down upon us with relentless fury. It was only then I realized that the absence of any detectable atmosphere in this region was the primary cause of our discomfort. On Earth, the blanket of air acted as an incubator against the sharp intensity of the sun's rays. Furthermore, the motion of the air in the form of winds also made for an equalization of temperature between places that were exposed to the direct glare from the sun and places that were sheltered. But here we had no such tempering influences. The rays of heat beat down mercilessly upon us.

"These outfits we're wearing aren't an awful lot of protection," grumbled Bob. His face visible through his helmet visor was flushed. Beads of perspiration stood out on his forehead.

"Not much," I agreed glumly. I extended my arm bearing the wristlet thermometer. "There, look…230° F…and that's the very limit of this instrument. Lord knows how much hotter it really is. That *tungstone* space suit you're wearing is not quite as good a protection against excessive heat as it is against excessive cold. But can you imagine where you and I would be without them?"

"Our little friends here don't seem to mind it at all." Bob looked about enviously at the escorting throng of creatures waddling along beside us and behind us. "Gosh, Earl, they don't seem to require protection from the sun's heat more than from the intense cold of night."

True enough; the cubical organisms appeared to be totally oblivious to the withering heat from above. They marched along blithely, chatting briskly with each other after their own peculiar fashion, waving their luminous bulbs cheerfully at us, trying to make us believe that they were enjoying themselves immensely.

Well, we finally came to a level plain that was set out in some kind of geometric pattern. Long straight ridges crossed and crisscrossed in accurate squares and rectangles. The ridges were mere lines of raised ground material only a few inches in height. Low, oddly shaped forms, also in severe geometric design and made of the same building substance, stood out here and there in the marked areas. These too were barely a foot in height. Throughout the plain there swarmed the cubical creatures, some moving from square to square, some clustered motionless along the ridges and about the raised geometric masses.

"This must be their city," I ventured.

"Well, it's the oddest city I've ever seen," observed Bob. "Where are the buildings, or streets, or anything else that you'd find in a centre of habitation?"

"Maybe they're underground," was my guess. But no, there were no traces of any openings in the ground, or any evidences that would indicate the existence of sub-surface dwellings. We wandered around among the squares and hexagons, stepping over ridges and traveling along what appeared to be streets and avenues.

And the natives were everywhere—a continuous streaming and eddying of gelatinous cubes in a geometric world. Our original escort from the rocket area had apparently melted into the general throngs. Evidently, we had been granted the freedom of the "City". As we wandered about the place, the creatures made way for us deferentially. They seemed to want to make us feel perfectly at home. One thing I soon observed. All through our roamings, I could perceive that *Red* and *Green* were near us always. I called my friend's attention to them. He had already become aware of the fact himself.

"Those two fellows certainly have become terribly attached to us," I said.

"Either that or else they've been detailed to keep an eye on us."

"That isn't very likely, Bob. They're acting more like a police escort to make our progress easier, than like a prison guard."

"Maybe so, but they surely were a great help in that rocket demonstration back, there."

"And now they're trying their best to see that our progress around these parts is smooth and unhampered. That's the simplest explanation of their being around us all of the time, isn't it?"

"Guess you're right, Earl! But...confound this heat!" It's getting worse and worse! Can't we find some shelter around here?"

There was nothing even remotely resembling shade anywhere in this vast valley. The low squares and oblongs of ground material that dotted the area were pitifully inadequate. They cast a series of thin shadows along their edges just about sufficient to afford shade to a small animal like a cat, provided the said cat was judicious enough to hug the side of the structure closely. The vegetation scattered about the valley was of the same stubby type we had seen elsewhere in this region—no more than a foot in height and woefully insufficient to protect us from the sizzling rays of the sun.

"I don't relish the idea of being roasted alive," observed Bob dryly; "No use...we'll have to find some kind of protection...even if we've got to build it ourselves...!"

He stopped short.

"Well, if that isn't an idea," he exclaimed. His flushed face beamed gleefully through his helmet window.

We were now off near the edge of the valley, and some distance away from the throngs and congestion that we had encountered in the centre of the city. Only a few of the natives were circulating about in our immediate vicinity. Even our trusty bodyguards, *Red* and *Green*, (if *bodyguards* we could call them) were for the moment busying themselves with some other occupation several hundred feet from our present position. "What's your idea?" I queried. "Why can't we rig up some temporary shed or something?" Bob replied eagerly. "Look!" He kicked the ground with the toe of his boat and dislodged one of the rubbery slabs of which the surface was composed. "Just the thing! We can stand some of those slices up on their edges, and then build a kind of shed. Gee, they come away easily! And light? Why they weigh hardly anything..."

Bob had stooped and pried up one of the flat plates of ground material. It was roughly square in shape, measuring about three feet on a side, and was nearly five inches thick. He balanced it on its edge, and then, seizing it with both hands, he raised the slab high over his head so as to form a roof.

"There! That's what we need. A—" The words suddenly died in his throat. A gasp of astonishment came feebly through my earphones. I looked at him fearfully. There he stood, feet spread far apart, arms stretched up and out, clutching the edges of the thick slice of ground material that formed a canopy above him. His head was thrown back, and his eyes were riveted on the substance.

"Well I'll be a..."

The exclamation was sliced short, and a low, drawn-out whistle of utter amazement came to my ears. Bob lowered the slab slowly until it rested edgewise on the ground. He peered at it intently first from one side, then from the other. Once more, an exclamation of astonishment escaped his lips. He raised the square plate aloft again, standing like a statue as before.

"For heaven's sake, what is it?" I queried sharply.

"Come here and take a look!" replied Bob tersely. "After which I wish you would please tell me if I'm going blind or nuts or what!"

He remained stationary, with the slab poised aloft. I was at his side in a jiffy. Standing close to him, I followed his gaze up at the substance above our heads. And now it was *my turn* to utter a sharp cry of amazement.

"Why Bob...it's...it's transparent!"

"Like a sheet of...of...*plate glass,"* added Bob, grimly.

He continued to hold the slab above our heads. We continued to look up at it and through it...yes, through it! There was the sun beating down mercilessly upon our upturned faces. There was the violet sky. There were the countless pinpoints of light that denoted stars and planets. All visible through this enigmatic substance picked up from beneath our feet.

Bob broke the spell.

"Now look at it," and he slowly lowered the rubbery slice. Bringing it down to the ground, he reversed it and placed it in exactly the same position from which he had lifted it only a few moments ago. Again, an exclamation of wonder and surprise burst from my throat. The material now looked just as it did before, dark, solid, opaque.

Again, Bob raised the slab over our heads, this time giving it a half turn as he lifted it, so that the surface which was formerly uppermost was now, in the elevated position, on bottom. We peered straight up at this surface...

Opaque as a board! My face felt a welcome coolness as the piercing rays from the sun were momentarily cut off.

"Of all the crazy things around here," I blurted out, "this is the *craziest!*"

"Crazy is no word for it," agreed Bob. He replaced the strange material very gingerly. "It's a clear case of one-way transparency!"

"And that's something nobody on Earth has ever seen. Just think of it, Bob! From one side, a sheet of clear plate glass...from the other side, a blank wall...!"

"Maybe we just happened to pick a strange piece. Let's try some others."

Bob fell to his knees and pried up a second slab, somewhat larger than the first. I busied myself with another portion some few feet away.

"This one's the same as the other," exclaimed my companion. He turned it over and over above his head. Meantime I had loosened my own plate of ground substance and tried it out for myself. It behaved exactly like the others. Bob and I were now feverishly excited. We forgot stifling heat, the eerie surroundings of this new world...everything. We dashed about energetically, ripping up portions of the scaly surface, some large, others small, and testing them out at various angles, both on the ground and held up aloft. Without a single exception the slices of spongy material all demonstrated the same phenomenal property—perfect opacity in one direction—perfect transparency in the opposite.

In the excitement of our extraordinary discovery, the cube men had been completely forgotten. They were suddenly brought back to our attention again. I looked up to find a swarm of them encircling us at our task. And they showed signs of agitation. They swayed and eddied about us nervously. The energetic motion of their luminous antennae bespoke their state of excitement. Bob and I paused in our investigation of the ground material.

"Looks like they're all steamed up about something," avowed my companion.

"Can it be that...?" I didn't finish my query. Bob had stooped to pry loose another section of surface substance. As he lifted it, one of the creatures nearest us disengaged himself from the encircling group and waddled up. His power appendage reached out and arrested the slice of matter in its upward progress. With gentle firmness, the substance was forced downward.

The next thing we knew, the section was back on the ground again. A vigorous agitation of the ring of pink bulbs that surrounded us gave evidence that the creatures approved of the mysterious action.

Bob and I looked at each other in bewilderment. "Seems as though they object to our meddling with this stuff," I whispered.

"Just to make sure," Bob replied grimly. He stooped again and clutched another slab. He hoisted it over his head with an air that closely resembled defiance. Foolhardy Bob. He always was that way...tempting the fates...

Well, nothing really serious happened—nothing more serious than a concussion like a clap of thunder—without the noise. As I shot back under the force of the blow, Bob went spinning around grotesquely, landing with a comical plop in a sitting position on the ground. The surface slab in question was back in its original spot. The cubical creature that had delivered the lightning blow stood apart from the rest of his fellows, swinging his orbs. They emitted a menacing glow...

"And that's *that!*" muttered my friend ruefully, as he picked himself up from his unconventional position and felt himself over his entire anatomy to see that he was all there. "The matter is definitely settled—and no question about it. These bugs object to our fooling around with their rubber plates. They don't want them pried loose—they don't even want them touched. And they mean business too! That's plain enough, isn't it?" and again he felt his person at the assorted tender spots which had resulted from his precipitous and unceremonious landing—and which would certainly have been more numerous and more tender save for the comparative softness of the medium on which he had landed.

We stopped our investigation of the ground material forthwith. The crowd of cube creatures relaxed. The air of ominous tenseness subsided. Again, we found ourselves meandering about the flattened area, while the streams of gelatinous organisms flowed and eddied about us. Momentarily we caught sight of *Red* and *Green.*

"I wonder if they took part in that little demonstration back there," I wondered out loud. "Did you see them, Bob?"

"Can't say that I did," he replied.

"They might have been around, but it was all over in such a flash, I didn't have a chance to observe much."

"Well, it doesn't really matter if they were there or not," I said. "They probably are of the same sentiment as all the rest. These beings must have some pretty strict beliefs about the sacredness of the ground they walk on—otherwise they wouldn't be so all-fired squeamish about anybody touching their old stuff."

"We'll have to look into the matter more fully later on." Bob's rejoinder was pregnant with hidden significance. "But meantime," he added, "I'm feeling right now as though I'm being boiled in oil."

As for my own sensations, I agreed with him heartily. The sun had been climbing steadily all the time. Its heat was now well nigh unbearable.

"We'd better get some relief right soon!" Bob continued, "or else there'll be a couple of the grandest cases of heat prostration that ever happened."

"There's only one way I can see out of it just now," I suggested. "And that is to get back to the ship."

"A great idea!" vouchsafed Bob enthusiastically. "Why didn't we think about it before? Come on...let's go!"

WE soon realized that we had no conception whatever as to the direction in which our ship lay. So many things had happened since we had emerged from the space flier to face the assembled cube creatures back there at our landing spot. We had journeyed to the site of the rocket dismemberment, and thence to this city of the plain. We had wandered about aimlessly for hours, and our sense of direction was completely awry.

Our bewilderment and increasing discomfort were plainly evident to the native organisms that eddied about us. Suddenly we espied our friends *Red* and *Green*. Bob waved to them and I joined the signaling. They pushed their way through the throng and presently were at our side. Brave fellows...and what intelligence too! We signaled our plight to them as best we could. I'd be willing to swear that they seemed to grasp the situation without any difficulty. The answering motions of their luminous tentacles replied as directly as could words—at least it looked that way to poor harassed Bob and me. If *Red* and *Green* had been present at the dramatic incident of the ground slabs, then they could readily have seen what we were aiming at, and could just-as readily see what we desired most right now—shelter from the scorching sun.

Whether or not they had been present then, they most certainly comprehended our situation now. There was no mistaking that flash of intelligence in their pink headlights.

The two fellows turned to the rest of the crowd and engaged them in vigorous conversation. Bob and I sagged against each other weakly, awaiting developments. Soon the confab was ended. Our two chromatic friends joined us again, one on each side, and beckoned us to march. We marched. And the entire flock of cube men came trooping after us.

Red and *Green* knew exactly where we wanted to be taken. We thanked a kind Providence for sending us two such intelligent creatures. On we tramped, with our guides beside us and the entire entourage trailing along behind. We reached the valley containing the dismembered rocket hulks, skirted it, and soon left it behind. Over ridges and through gullies, up and down ever the undulating surface of slabs…slabs…nothing but slabs. My senses were beginning to reel, my steps faltered. The stifling heat was now well nigh unbearable. I felt Bob catch up my sagging body. I rallied somewhat and staggered on. And then…

There was our space flier, lying just where we had left it. We stumbled along, with my friend now half dragging me most of the way. Ages seemed to elapse before we reached No. 43. The escorting creatures stood by deferentially, with *Red* and *Green* at the head. More ages struggled by while Bob fumbled with the door mechanism. All I could do was to lean feebly against the side of the vessel and gasp for breath. The hatch was open at last. We stumbled in, with a last grateful wave to our escort. Once through the inner door panel I tore at my helmet and space suit and flung it far from me. Bob wasn't wasting a moment in doing likewise. We sank onto a couple of seats and gasped for breath.

"Whew, this is a relief!" panted my friend, as he mopped a dripping brow. For the moment, I hadn't enough strength to utter a word. All I could do was fan myself weakly with nothing more effective than the palm of my hand.

"I don't see how we could have stood that withering heat much longer," said Bob. He threw his head back, stretched out his legs and relaxed luxuriously in the refreshing coolness of the ship's interior.

"Darned if I know how *they* stand it!" I found my voice again, although a pitifully weak one. "The heat doesn't bother them at all." I jerked a finger at the nearest window. Luminous knobs were swaying against it, and varicolored cubical masses were pressed close to the transparent surface. The other windows had their quotas of native organisms. Were they waving cheery greetings to us? Were they expressing their regrets at the extreme discomfort that we were experiencing in their cherished climate? Were they offering apologies to us for that bit of momentary harshness to us in connection with the dislodged ground plates? Whatever their message was, it certainly was not one of hostility.

We waved back cheerfully—if a trifle weakly. One by one the creatures dropped away from the windows. The last to remain were our trusty guides, *Red* and *Green.* They held on for a last lingering look together, and then, with a final wave of their appendages, they slid smoothly out of sight.

A FEW hours of refreshing sleep in the delicious coolness of our ship's quarters worked wonders for both of us. With all the exciting things that had been happening to us ever since we had put foot in this bizarre region, the thought of food had left us completely. It now came back to us almost simultaneously, and with an unquenchable urge. We dined (maybe it was *lunched*—or was it *breakfasted?)* with extreme gusto.

"It all seems like a dream," I remarked, exhaling vast clouds of cigarette smoke into the confined area of the chamber. Bob was lolling on his bunk, likewise erupting billows of smoke with luxurious abandon. Thanks to our efficient air purification system, the atmosphere within the compartment was maintained in a fairly breathable condition. After the recent long spell in the stifling confinement of our space helmets, almost anything in the way of atmosphere was acceptable.

"Well, Earl, dream or no dream, here's something that's *real!*" Bob rose from his reclining position. He glanced first through the nearest window. I followed his glance. A handful of waddling creatures were in sight, moving about aimlessly at a distance from the ship. None were visibly close to us. Bob nodded with an air of satisfaction, and hastened over to the corner of the room where he had flung his space suit. He fumbled about for a moment and from one of its pockets he hauled forth an object. He brought it out into the light, keeping over to one side of the room, so as not to be visible through the windows. He held it up. It was a small slab of ground substance.

"I managed to pinch it while no one was looking," Bob whispered, glancing about apprehensively, as though momentarily expecting that lightning-like blow that had tumbled him over in so undignified a manner back there in the city of the plain. The contraband object was about four inches square and about two inches in thickness. Bob turned it over and over between his fingers. He held it up toward the single bulb in the ceiling, rotating it slowly first on one axis, then on another. I watched with extreme fascination. Now the bulb's rays burst through clear and strong; now they were blotted out from view. The fragment exhibited that same mystifying one-way transparency that was characteristic of all the slabs which we had tested so feverishly back on the plain.

Bob studied the material minutely. "Look, Earl," he remarked, "how crystal clear it is in this position…and also in this position…in fact whenever the light is shining down on its upper surface, no matter at what angle. And now, edgewise...no, it's totally opaque, just as opaque as when I turn it over completely and let the light hit the side which was underneath before. So it looks as though this stuff, if it were in the form of a cube, would be perfectly transparent when the light hits only one of its six faces. A darned peculiar substance..."

I agreed with Bob. It certainly resembled nothing that either of us had ever seen on Earth.

"And notice this Earl," he continued. He held the material for a minute or so close to the surface of the small electric heater built into the wall just above the floor level. He removed it momentarily, and then brought it back again to its position near the heater. The warming rays burst forth to my outstretched palm with unvarying intensity, regardless of whether or not the substance was interposed.

"Showing," added Bob, "that the stuff is just as transparent to *heat rays* as it is to *light rays*, provided the rays strike on the upper surface, or rather the surface that was on top when I picked it up from the ground."

"And now, getting back to the matter of *light* once more," Bob went on, "this material, even in its perfectly transparent position, doesn't follow the common behavior of transparent substances...it doesn't *refract* light." He held the small slab down against the page of an open magazine. The type stood out boldly and clearly through the two-inch thickness. There was none of the customary distortion and bending of the light rays that is evident when one looks through a refracting plate of glass.

I took the extraordinary substance in my hand. Although I had picked up and examined half a dozen or more slabs back in the cube men's city, I was struck for the first time by its unearthly lightness. "It weighs much less than the lightest wood I've ever handled," I mused. "And look, Bob, it's not the least bit porous...as solid as a chunk of metal."

"Let's try a simple specific gravity test," and Bob procured a can of water. I dropped the substance into it. The slab remained afloat high and dry. "Holy smoke!" exclaimed Bob. "It's flat on the surface of the water, with practically none of it submerged."

And to be sure, the slice of ground material rested on the water as though the latter were frozen solid. It floated in much the same manner as a block of wood would float in a dish of mercury.

"Then its specific gravity," guessed Bob, "must be in the neighborhood of *point zero-zero something* I should say that in its relative weight it more nearly resembles a gas than either a *solid or a liquid"*

At this moment, a sudden scraping noise on the surface of the ship halted our experimentation. Bob hastily snatched the telltale specimen from the can of water and concealed it under a sheaf of sky maps on the table. Several gelatinous bodies appeared at the window over our heads. Among them, we recognized *Green*. The creatures waved cheerfully at us. We waved back with equal cheerfulness.

"They must be extremely anxious about our comfort," said Bob.

"Or else very suspicious of our movements," I added sententiously.

Again, the cubical organisms slid from view, and we relaxed. Bob carefully hid away the smuggled slab in one of the wall lockers. We resumed our smoking in profound contemplation. Bob broke the silence after a few minutes—and he broke it with a bang.

"I've got it, Earl!" he exploded, and he leaped from his seat and leaned toward me eagerly. "It's as clear as day!"

"It's as clear as mud to *me,"* I puffed, my mental processes working with their habitual slowness, I must confess.

"From the moment that we landed her," continued Bob, "I had a sort of sneaking notion about the correct explanation of this whole mysterious business. My ideas have been clarifying themselves right along during all our activities and in our so-called adventures around these parts. And now I guess I have it all pieced together, just like a jigsaw puzzle. Here's the way I see it:

"This region must be part of a vast layer like an eggshell that encircles the Earth at the outer limits of the atmosphere. This shell is composed of an extremely light and perfectly transparent material. How thick this shell is, I have no way of guessing. But it cannot be very thick, because the six rocketships, and then our own, burst through without any great difficulty, or any serious damage to themselves. How this layer of matter ever came to be formed here I won't even attempt to guess. But it's here—no doubt about that. And its one-way transparency makes it completely invisible from below. That's why the existence of any such shell has always been a secret. Astronomers for ages have looked at it and through it. They've made all kinds of observations about the planets, stars, constellations, galaxies and other celestial phenomena without for a moment suspecting that anything lay as close to the Earth as this shell. Now how does the whole story strike you, Earl?"

"Darned clever explanation," I admitted. "But let's look into it a little. What does the Earth get from outer space? First, there's the light and heat energy from the sun. No doubt, these rays break through the thing you call a shell without any trouble, I guess your recent tests prove that matter conclusively. Then there are the cosmic rays. What about them?"

"Well, if the cosmic rays originate somewhere far away in outer space, then they are certainly able to break through the shell, because they are easily detectable on Earth. Whether they penetrate with their full intensity, or whether they lose something while passing through is another story. I won't venture an opinion."

"But wait, Bob, here's something you can't get away from. What about *meteors?* Everybody knows that they fall through space and become luminous when they strike the Earth's atmosphere. Which means they first have to break through the shell, eh?"

"I've been puzzling about the question of meteors, and I guess that's the only explanation. They must plunge through the comparatively thin shell and continue their drop without any great reduction in speed. My guess is that this shell material offers very little resistance to an object passing through it. After all, Earl, there are the spaceships that sailed up from below. Do you remember the sensation when we hit the shell? Like flying through a layer of soft cheese, wasn't it?"

"But, if the meteors fall through, there must be some holes or openings left by their passage. That's logical, isn't it, Bob?"

"Logical enough, but I'll admit we haven't come across any yet. Still, Earl, we couldn't locate any hole made by our own passage through, or any caused by the other rocketships. Maybe this peculiar ground material has a way of folding back again and covering up any opening made by a body shooting through. By George, anything at all is possible here! Now take for example this question: What holds up this thin shell of matter at a distance of 130 miles or so from the Earth's surface? Why doesn't it come crashing down like a house built of cards? All we can do is guess. This stuff, being so extremely light, doesn't need a very great force to keep it up. Maybe it's some mysterious backpressure from the Earth's atmosphere, or some ingredient in it that balances the weight of the shell. Maybe it's tied up with the rubbery material itself—some anti-gravitational effect or something...I'm sure I don't know, Earl."

"Well, Bob, I've got to admit that your explanation, even though it sounds like a fantastic pipe dream, seems to be a mighty good one. I'll be darned if I'm not beginning to believe it myself. It certainly fits in with all the observed facts. And now about these cube creatures. They deserve a word of explanation too, don't they?"

"A mighty interesting and curious form of organic development is what I'd call them. They probably have evolved through countless ages to their present form. No doubt Nature has discovered that this particular physical state must be ideal for carrying on life under the peculiar conditions existing here on the shell."

"I'd say that these beings have a pretty tough time of it, even at best. There is first the absence of any atmosphere. Then there is the problem of water...have you seen any yet, Bob? I haven't observed a trace. Goodness knows what they use for food. Furthermore, there are the terrible extremes of temperature which they must endure. And then what of the murderous pelting they must get by, the cosmic rays that are constantly striking their unprotected shell? And last, but by no means least, have you considered what even a moderate meteor shower would do to them? They must be bombarded by hundreds of meteors every day...and not a chance to protect themselves as far as we've been able to see. At least we on Earth have our atmosphere which acts as a blanket to shield us from the effect of meteors. But these poor shell people must be a constant prey to them. By the way, I wonder, Bob, why we haven't seen any meteors yet."

"Fortunately this particular time is not one of very great meteoric activity. Even so, there must be plenty of those visitors from the skies raining down upon the poor inhabitants of this eggshell of matter. I suspect that if we stay around much longer we're going to encounter some of them sooner or later. Yet, in spite of the apparent danger to which the shell natives are exposed, I'm willing to wager that they have discovered some means of protecting themselves from meteors."

"Whichever way you look at it, they're a remarkable race. Think of their advanced intelligence, the mastery of tremendous forces by means of their powerful bulb attachments. Think of their methods of communication. I even believe they are able to read our thoughts. Their progress in scientific development must be considerable. We haven't seen any of their achievements along those lines yet, but there certainly must be evidences. Just consider how neatly they dismantled those six ships. And remember their curiosity as to how the rocket mechanism worked. We've got to admit, Bob, that they're a mighty remarkable people."

"I wonder what their reaction was to this sudden invasion from below. After all, Earl, just consider how our people down on Earth would take it if a number of bizarre objects would suddenly shoot up from beneath our feet in the way that our ships did up here. No doubt the local inhabitants must believe that their shell is solid—that is assuming that this thing we're standing on is not a mere fragment in space, but a continuous unbroken shell extending completely around our Earth. Certainly they have no conception of an entire planet swimming in the centre of their shell."

"Swimming is the word, Bob. And it just occurred to me...the shell must follow the rotational motion of the Earth on its axis, because we have the same succession of sunrise and sunset, with about the same intervals of day and night as on Earth—although, with the lack of any atmosphere you wouldn't exactly call the period when the sun is visible day, would you?"

"I wouldn't be at all surprised if the cube people are so far advanced in science that they actually know as much astronomy as we do...maybe more, because they have so much of a better chance to view the heavens than our Earth-bound astronomers have with that thick blanket of atmosphere always in the way. Very likely the shell inhabitants are familiar with the solar system, in fact, they may believe their territory to be the planet that we have always known as the third from the sun."

"By George, the thing sounds more fantastic the more we analyze the whole matter. Yet undoubtedly it's all as true as gospel truth itself."

"To me it sounds like a Jules Verne story. I remember reading a tale written by him about a trip made to the centre of the Earth...do you remember it? It told of a journey through an extinct crater in Iceland and the discovery of a vast world laying below in much the same manner as our own Earth lies below the shell upon which we now are."

"Yes, I remember the story well. That exploration trip was a sort of reverse procedure from our own."

"Talking about *reverse,* what about this reverse transparency up here? That's probably the most puzzling fact in the whole puzzling situation. I guess you've heard the story about the new maid who cleaned the windows thoroughly on the inside but purposely left them dirty on the outside so that those snoopy kids next door couldn't look in. Well, here we have just what that good servant girl was striving for...one-way transparency."

"I wonder if the shell people are aware of the peculiarity of their ground substance. Perhaps they do know about it, which may help to explain why they were so thoroughly against our tampering with the stuff."

"And another thing...the ground may be perfectly transparent and therefore invisible from below, but how about the creatures themselves—do they follow the same rule of directional visibility? If they don't, then they should be visible from the Earth through telescopes. Isn't that so?"

"Quite right, the only way to find that out is to try looking at one of them from below. I dare say we'd find the same one-sided transparency. But even if we didn't, remember that the individual creature, himself, is nothing more than a blob of colored jelly, which is nearly transparent. And, at this great distance from the Earth, even the most powerful telescope wouldn't be able to detect him—or even a large number of them grouped together."

"Well, if the shell men are not visible from below, how about you and me? We certainly must stand out clear and bold against the sky."

"Yes...like a couple of minute specks, perhaps...that is, if those on Earth knew just where to train their instruments."

"And what about the rocketships? They should be even more distinct than we are, shouldn't they?"

"Right! Provided, again, the telescopes were pointed straight at them. However, considering the great distance, and the comparative minuteness of ourselves and the space flyers, I don't think we stand much chance of being spotted."

OUR conversation rambled along in this manner for what might have been several hours. We had no conception of the flight of time. The sudden discovery of the probable state of affairs, together with all the mulling over of notes and assorted data, and the general coordination of observations, theories, conjectures, facts and near facts occupied our attention to the exclusion of everything else. We might even have forgotten the group of cubical organisms patrolling the vicinity of our ship, if it were not for an occasional glimpse of them through our windows.

There was no use in our venturing out again in the intense heat of the sun. We lounged around, ate again, took turns at napping, and then continued our discourse of which there never seemed to be any end in sight. The whole series of phenomena was too wonderful and too mystifying to be dispatched in anything short of a solid week of discussion, we thought.

Our plan was to emerge once more after the sun had set, and the outside temperature was more bearable. By that time, we had taken stock of our situation pretty thoroughly, and had determined on some concrete plan of action. Our chief aim must now be to learn as much about the shell and its inhabitants as our limited stay would permit. We must at the same time make an effort to repair the ship so as to assure us a means of returning to Earth. As to our supplies of food and oxygen, they were sufficient to keep us for several weeks if necessary. We determined to take full advantage of the time at our disposal to explore the shell, either on foot, or, better yet, by means of the rocketship, if we could repair the latter. Bob even mentioned the possibility of putting one of the smaller flyers in shape and using that for reconnoitering expeditions. Of course, we agreed, that was contingent on how much fuel we could manage to scrape together from the tanks of all the ships. Unless there was an abundance of *benzite,* we could not afford to waste any. Our return trip was of paramount importance.

Before we left the ship again we tried something that we hadn't attempted yet, namely to establish communication with the Earth. After all, we had completely forgotten that when we took off from the Earth's surface we left behind us an ocean of suspense and expectation. Throughout our climb into the upper atmosphere, we had maintained an interrupted contact with the New York station of Stratosphere Transport. Then came our dramatic burst through the shell and into this new world. Communication had ceased abruptly. And now there must be a seething turmoil down below as a result of our disappearance into space. Or else, perhaps Bob and I had already been accepted as martyrs in the cause of scientific progress, and had been by this time crossed off the records.

An investigation of the condition of our radio apparatus soon blasted our hopes. I discovered that the transmitter had been badly damaged by the initial impact of the ship. Although there was a possibility of affecting some makeshift repairs, we soon realized that they would take time.

"Just think!" said Bob with deep chagrin and disappointment. "Here we are at a distance of 130 odd miles from New York—closer to the big city than if we were in Albany—and we're as isolated as though we were on the surface of the moon."

"There must be *some* way," I replied thoughtfully. "*Some* method by which we could let our friends down below know we are safe and inform them of our discoveries up here on the shell."

"There's one way," suggested Bob. "If we knew that the shell was not too thick, we could dig a hole and drop a message."

"That's an idea," I replied with enthusiasm, "provided we could do it without letting the cube people catch us at it. You know how they feel about our molesting the surface of their ground." My enthusiasm slowly ebbed. "It doesn't look as though we'd have much chance of accomplishing that—those creatures seem to be right on our tails morning, noon, and night." I glanced through the window at the cluster of gelatinous creatures maintaining their patient vigil very close by.

After sundown, Bob and I donned our *tungstone* suits and helmets and emerged once more into the realm of the shell men. Curiously enough, their numbers had dwindled considerably during the time we had been sheltering ourselves in the spaceship. A mere handful of them were there to greet us as we hopped out upon the rubbery ground. And among them, to be sure, we singled out the ever-present *Red* and *Green*. These two creatures appeared to act with some sort of authority over the remainder of the group.

"I guess our two friends have succeeded in getting themselves appointed commanding officers in our bodyguard," laughed Bob. He waved a cheery greeting to the group, and we received an equally cheery response from *Red* and *Green*.

Bob signaled to them that we desired to be escorted back to the scene of the rocketship dismantling, for our first consideration was a speedy repair job on our vessel. I must admit that Bob's method of conveying this message was indeed crude—I'm sure that my own would have been no better. However, our two friends seemed to comprehend instantly, and started off in the proper direction at a pace as swift as was commensurate with their waddling motion. Bob and I followed hurriedly. The remaining shell creatures took up the rear.

"A pair of first rate helpers." I remarked. "If ever we need the services of a couple of loyal and intelligent assistants we can depend on them. I'd even be willing to bet that, in their attachment to us, they could stop at nothing, even if it were in opposition to the will of the rest of their countrymen."

"We may yet find them to be of vital importance in the working out of our plans for the immediate future," said Bob with deep significance. He did not make any effort to amplify his cryptic statement. The matter was dropped for the time being, by reason of a sudden development that burst upon us with dramatic swiftness and intensity.

We had put barely a quarter of a mile between the ship and ourselves, when the escorting group of cubical beings stopped dead in their tracks. There was a momentary flashing of their luminous appendages, a nervous, uneasy swaying of pink bulbs, as though they detected an unspoken warning of danger in the space about us. *Red* and *Green* appeared as frightened as the rest.

We halted abruptly and glanced about fearfully. What new manifestation was to be expected in this strange region of the unexpected?

"Looks like something is going to happen," muttered Bob grimly—and real soon too!" We clung close to each other and waited…

We did not have long to wait…perhaps not even twenty seconds…and then it happened…with a bang!

A HUGE dark mass loomed suddenly above us, and came down with a furious impact not fifty feet from us. There was no sound of course, but the vibrations of the crash came rumbling through my feet and resounded throughout my entire body like a thunderclap. Bob and I were thrown violently to the ground, just as another dark mass, this one smaller than the first, came hurtling down on the other side of us about the same distance away.

"Meteors!" came Bob's frantic yell in my helmet phones. He scrambled to his feet only to be thrown down in a heap on top of me by the landing of two or three other masses. In each case, the meteor whizzed through space with breath-taking velocity, struck the soft ground, and disappeared completely underneath. The shell surface seemed to open up for a split second, and then close again instantly, to swallow

The shell surface seemed to open up for a split second, and then close again instantly, to swallow the fragments without leaving a trace.

the fragments without leaving a trace. Large and small masses now began to rain down in earnest. By the sheerest miracle, none of them fell close enough to do us any harm. We pulled each other to a standing position. The shell creatures were thoroughly demoralized. Some were waddling around in a wild panic. Others were rooted motionless to the ground in abject terror. A few shapeless gelatinous masses scattered on the ground denoted real casualties. As for *Red* and *Green*, they appeared no calmer than their panic-stricken fellow creatures.

As if by instinct, Bob and I turned in the direction of our vessel which we had quit only a few minutes ago. Bob beckoned wildly to the disorganized group of shell beings to follow us. They were too terror-stricken to comprehend or to obey.

"Come on, Earl!" he shouted hoarsely. We plunged up the slope toward the ship. As we ran, it occurred to me in a vague sort of way that our vessel was a pitifully inadequate protection against the murderous rain of death from the skies. A direct hit by even a moderately sized meteoric fragment would squash the flyer as if it were a mere eggshell. However, such is the comforting philosophy of a drowning man clutching at a straw, that we ran on as though the ship spelled absolute salvation to us.

The huge missiles continued to drop all about us. Why our dramatic adventure was not ended then and there by one of the flying masses I cannot to this day understand. Certainly, we must have been endowed by a kind providence with a substantial pair of charmed lives. For the third time now we fell precipitously through the doorway of our vessel and tumbled into the interior. It was getting to be a habit for us to leave our quarters simply and unceremoniously, and return to them with a huge bang.

Once inside, we stationed ourselves at one of the windows, watching the havoc of the meteoric hailstorm without, and fervently praying that none of the fragments decided to come our way.

After what seemed hours, although it really must have been only two or three minutes at the most, the meteors stopped falling. The terrific rumbling and vibration was supplanted by a deathlike calm. Bob and I looked at each other through our helmet visors with immense relief. In the excitement of the moment, we found ourselves still wearing the full space regalia, just as we had burst through from outdoors.

"Another close shave," I whispered in awe. "Just imagine what one of those lumps could have done to us!" I shuddered at the thought.

"Right now," replied Bob earnestly, "the question is what these lumps have done to our party of friends outside."

Again, we passed through the air lock and stepped out upon the ground. I looked about. Except for a few craterlike circular ridges, and here and there, several fragments of surface slabs that had become dislodged or warped, there was no tangible evidence of the recent hail of death.

As we stood there contemplating the scene, a bedraggled group of shell men came toward us from around the other side of the ship. *Red* and *Green* were among them as they waddled painfully in our direction. From the energetic motion of their luminous antennae, despite the grave injuries that some of the creatures had obviously suffered, it was evident that they were happy that Bob and I had been spared. Looking off down the slope we could see a half dozen still forms lying scattered over the ground—victims of a ruthless destruction from the skies. It was clear that, with all the remarkable development and truly super-human progress accomplished by these denizens of the shell world, they had as yet developed no protection against this inexorable scourge from above.

SEVERAL eventful days passed—days crowded with activity and with new experiences. I should really say *nights* and not *days*. We were by no means anxious to repeat that first spell of torture under the merciless sun. One taste was sufficient. Therefore, Bob and I remained judiciously within the shelter of the ship during the period of greatest heat, and ventured out only after sunset. On the approach of dawn, we hurried back to the welcome protection of the flyer.

The shell people were now fully accustomed to our presence in their domain. For a day or two, we usually found ourselves with a whole retinue of escorting creatures, some leading us, some trailing us, all eager to be of service. Then the numbers dwindled, as the novelty of our presence wore off. Soon we could count only a dozen or less who clung to us. Finally, we found ourselves traveling about with only two creatures as our personal escort—and of course, these two were none other than that indefatigable pair, *Red* and *Green*.

They conducted us through their cities—we soon found that the geometrically designed area on the plain was only one of a series of such structural developments. I term them cities, for want of any better name. Our two faithful guides took us to the outlying districts of their domain, where we saw for the first time the sources of food upon which the shell race depended for their sustenance. Here, as far as the eye could reach, were rows upon rows of foot-high vegetation, being tended by gangs of cubical workers. We watched other groups of shell creatures transporting the crops from the fields back to the cities on huge slabs of surface material that they guided deftly over the ground. It was positively uncanny to see these conveyances, supported by nothing tangible from below, gliding smoothly and swiftly a few inches above the surface. Only a touch here and there from the luminous knobs of the attending crew was sufficient to steer the massive bulk of the slab and the freight that it bore. What the motive power was we could not fathom, but we decided between ourselves that it was most certainly associated with those mysterious appendages of whose power we had seen so many evidences.

It was interesting to note that, in all the manipulation of the slices of ground material, they were seldom raised more than six inches from the surface, and in no case was a slab ever supported in any other way except strictly parallel to its original position on the ground.

"It must be part of their very religion," remarked Bob as we stood with our two friends on a slight elevation, watching the proceedings down in the fields. "On that point they certainly made things unmistakably clear to us when we attempted to play around with those sections of surface material. To turn a slice over on its back must be the most serious taboo on their calendar. No wonder they made such a fuss over it." Instinctively Bob rubbed his body ruefully where he had been most sorely chastised on that memorable occasion.

Only rarely during these few days were we troubled by meteors. It was fortunate. Bob explained that this happened to be a period of diminished meteoric activity. In all cases, the speeding missiles struck at great distances from us. In fact, we began to become accustomed to them, just as seasoned soldiers in a trench become inured to the ceaseless bombardment of high explosive shells. We just ducked our heads automatically, and went on with the particular task in hand.

After a few days of what one might call sightseeing, Bob and I turned our attention to real business. We made a careful survey of the dismantled rocket vehicles. Bob picked out a number of the essential parts required for the repair of our own driving mechanism, and had them transported to the ship. As far as the actual handling of the parts was concerned, Bob and I scarcely had to raise a finger. Merely a sign from us, and a dozen cubical beings were right on the job to do the manual labor, with *Red* and *Green* in the roles of general foreman of the gang.

We soon learned that haste was essential. We had observed previously that the dismantling processes, as carried on by the shell workers before our arrival on the scene, had been done with neatness and care, so as to preserve the mechanism as far as possible. However, the frequent invasion of meteors had wrecked serious damage to some of the projectiles as we may call them and their mechanisms. We further discovered, to our vast dismay, that the falling fragments had also smashed several of the auxiliary containers and had scattered our reserve fuel supply over a wide area.

"This will never do," my friend remarked grimly. "I'm afraid our stay up here on the shell will have to be cut short very materially. A few more meteors dropping on this spot will completely wipe out our chance of ever getting back to Earth again."

We plunged into the task with renewed vigor. Our cubical assistants seemed to sense the meaning of our feverish activity. Perhaps they reasoned that we were planning another demonstration like the one to which we had treated them shortly after our arrival on the shell. At any rate, they fell to the task with doubled energy. It was no easy job, but slowly we saw it nearing completion. Bob was a veritable wizard in fitting parts together that never were made to fit together, and patching up a seemingly hopeless wreck, with a conglomeration of fittings stolen from a half dozen equally hopeless wrecks.

Nearly a week had now passed. Bob and I were in the combined control room, living quarters and sleeping chamber of No 43. We were discussing the plans of our getaway—I use *getaway* advisedly, because we could see that a more prolonged stay would place us in a very precarious position, principally on account of the serious depletion in our oxygen supply. If we could but establish some form of communication with the world a hundred and thirty odd miles beneath our feet then, we reasoned, our position would not be so terrifying. We could send news of the strange realm that we had discovered, and direct the dispatching of other parties with the necessary supplies and equipment to engage in extensive exploration of the shell.

Yet, all avenues for communicating with our fellow beings seemed to be closed to us. My repeated efforts at putting the ship's radio into temporary working order seemed fruitless. That method was barred, apparently. Several times we discussed the idea of finding some opening in the rubbery surface through which we could drop a message, and we took every opportunity while on our trip about, to try to locate some such hole, made either by one of the rocketships coming through from below, or by a meteor falling from the skies. Here again our efforts proved unproductive. To try to dig our own shaft seemed to be a hopeless task. What with the indeterminate thickness of the shell, as well as the obvious hostility of the native organisms at any attempt of ours to molest the surface slabs, that plan was out of the question.

"I've got a great idea!" Bob suddenly burst forth with boyish enthusiasm. "Now why didn't we think of it before?"

"Quick, Bob," I urged, "what's your latest? Spill it!"

"It would be a great stunt, Earl," he continued absently, "provided..."

"Provided what?"

"Provided the shell people could be made to look somewhere else long enough for us to do something with their ground slabs."

"That part of your idea doesn't look promising at all...but what's the scheme?"

"Well, simply, it's this: The surface slices are, of course, transparent in one direction, and therefore visible from above, but transparent and invisible when viewed from below. Now if we could secretly turn over one of these slabs without being bothered by the natives, then that particular section would become visible when seen from underneath. Ah, I see that you're beginning to comprehend the idea..."

The light of understanding was starting to dawn on me. Darn clever notion I thought...

"So you see, Earl, if we could turn over a sufficiently large number of these slices, and put them together to spell out some kind of simple message, then our people below would see it as a dark inscription against the sky, and clearly legible."

A moment's thought made it evident to both of us almost simultaneously that Bob's scheme, however original and ingenious it might be, was doomed to failure even before it could be attempted.

"It's no use," I shook my head gloomily. "The idea isn't practicable—at least not the way we're situated right now. In the first place we'd have to make each letter of our message enormously large, and even the simplest inscription would have to extend over a tremendous area."

"And in the second place," added Bob dejectedly, "we'd just about have one slab turned over by the time these infernal shell people would be right on us—and that's as far as we'd ever get."

"That's just it, Bob. Even if we *could* manage to sneak away to some obscure spot and try to construct this message of reversed ground slabs, we wouldn't be able to keep it secret very long. No...I'm afraid that idea is definitely out..."

"Maybe so!" Bob burst forth with sudden fervor. "Nevertheless I'm game to try it—no matter how crazy the scheme might sound. We're up against it, Earl, and there aren't many things left for us to try—this is one of them, and we've got to give it a chance. These shell people haven't been watching us very closely of late. If we could skip off to some out-of-the-way place, we might get away with it. Even if we don't spell out a complete message, at least we might construct a word, or maybe only a letter or two—anything at all—just to let the people on Earth know that we're up here safe and sound—or at least comparatively so."

"Well Bob," I laughed, "your present scheme is just as scatterbrained as all the others that you've cooked up in your day, even to the scheme of this entire trip itself. The chances are a thousand to one against us, but if you say so, then we'll go ahead and try it. Let's go..."

Buoyantly, although with full conviction that our mission was a hopeless one, we donned our space suits and emerged into the star-domed splendor of a typical shell night. Those inexorable shadows of ours. *Red* and *Green* were waiting for us.

Bob and I stopped in our tracks and looked at each other in dismay. Here was something we had forgotten to take into account. How to get rid of this persistent couple!

"We certainly can't do anything with them around," I said.

"They don't seem to understand that there are times when we crave a little privacy," replied Bob peevishly.

"Maybe we can give them the slip," I suggested. "Let's put up a stiff pace."

We started off down the slope. Each step was a prodigious leap that took us sailing up a dozen feet in space and landed us thirty feet away. The legendary "Seven League Boots" had nothing on this! I felt giddy at the phenomenal pace.

When we had covered about a half mile, I turned. *Red* and *Green* were directly behind us, their lower appendages vibrating briskly over the ground, their luminous antennae glowing and waving joyfully. I clutched my chum's arm.

"This is uncanny, Bob!"

"No more uncanny than anything else up here!" was his panting reply.

We started off once more at a killing stride. Our shadows were right there on our heels! There was no shaking them off. Either they had means of attaching themselves to us by some invisible force, so that they trailed along in our wake with no effort on their part, or else *Red* and *Green* possessed faculties of locomotion that were absent in the rest of the shell people.

Bob and I sat down to ponder this new situation. The two persistent shell creatures hovered close by, like a couple of faithful hounds.

"They just won't be shaken, Bob."

"That's very evident. Guess we've got to give up my pet scheme."

"Why not go through with it, regardless of the presence of *Red* and *Green*?"

"We might do that, Earl, but there's hardly a chance they'll let us get away with it, even though they seem to be stuck on us so."

"It can't hurt to try."

Again we started off, this time at a more moderate gait, with the two "unshakable" organisms just a few steps behind us. Here and there, we passed groups of shell people going about their particular tasks. They paid scant attention to us, even though our haste might seem to be unusual. Our presence in the shell world was now more or less taken for granted. So that any activity in which, we might happen to be engaged would appear to them as matter of fact and commonplace.

About an hour of tramping over the rubbery surface brought us to a region which was more isolated than any we had so far seen. While covering the last mile or more we encountered only two or three lone cube creatures. And now there was not a single one in sight, with the exception of the inevitable *Red* and *Green* trailing along behind us.

"This looks like a good spot," I suggested.

Bob bent down and dislodged a medium sized slab. I stood by apprehensively with a watchful eye on the two shell men. They did not budge from their positions. Bob straightened up as he heaved the ground section on one of its edges, but still no sign from *Red* and *Green.* I seized a corner of the slab and helped Bob ease it over flat on its other surface. All was quiet on the shell front!

My chum and I looked at each other in amazement. This was certainly unlike the hectic experience we had had on that other occasion.

"Well this beats all!" I whispered into my helmet transmitter. "Either the shell people have suffered a complete change of heart, or else…"

Bob had stooped to disengage another ground slice when suddenly *Red* and *Green* sprang forward in unison. Bob was almost bowled over by the suddenness of the move.

Instinctively I flung my arms up for protection from the precipitous lunge.

Imagine our astonishment when the two shell creatures seized the partly raised ground section and brought it over deftly on its back. That task accomplished they turned to the adjacent portion and heaved that one over with neatness and dispatch. Then, came a third slab and another while Bob and I looked on in speechless bewilderment. *Red* and *Green* now halted and faced us, as though awaiting further orders.

"Well, I'm a fried onion!" breathed Bob in an awed tone. "They're actually helping us...imagine, Earl, *actually helping us!*"

"I can't make it out, Bob!" I replied. "These two creatures are here for us no matter what we do, and no matter how much it may run counter to the customs and beliefs of their countrymen. Strange bugs, these!"

"Well, Earl," spoke up my chuni quickly, "now's our chance to make hay while the sun shines. No matter what's back of it all, this much is certain: We can spell out our message here without being molested…in fact with the advantage of some welcome assistance from our good friends here."

We fell to work eagerly, and began a systematic reversing of surface plates. The possibilities of our success had appeared so remote at the time we had set forth on this message-sending expedition that we had made no clear-cut plans as to what message to send. Automatically, however, we commenced the laying of a line of slabs as nearly straight as we could. That would mark the beginning of some clearly defined symbol, we decided. As each section was turned over and placed on its back, its neighbor seemed to melt away, to become invisible, revealing the ground surface directly below it.

Looking down from above there appeared to be nothing very striking about the line of reversed slabs. But I could picture how it looked from below—a thin dark line slowly growing longer as its message was being written against the sky. Of course, it would be invisible at night, but with the coming of day, it ought to stand out boldly for the Earth people to read. However, the dark line would no doubt be too thin to be seen clearly at such a distance. We must make it much wider, by turning over a larger area of ground slabs. So Bob and I talked and planned as we busied ourselves with the strange task which we had started. *Red* and *Green* were right there by our side, lifting and reversing slab after slab with enthusiastic abandon. If only we could continue the work unmolested. If only…

A low cry in my earpiece halted me in my work. I straightened up with a ground slab in my arms, and wheeled around to Bob. He was facing away from me and pointing. I followed his outstretched arm. A cube man was approaching our spot in a precipitous hurry. His glowing knobs were waving angrily, and even his very body gave forth a dim phosphorescence in his extreme agitation. He came straight for me and lunged forth with one of his appendages. The surface slab which I was holding was torn from my grip and I was sent spinning to one side. I regained my balance with difficulty.

Meantime another shell creature had sprung into existence, apparently from nowhere. He joined his fellow, and together they fell to work returning the dislodged ground plates back to their original positions. Three more creatures hove into view and pitched in with vigor. Seemingly indifferent to the presence of *Red* and *Green*, the intruding creatures bent to their task industriously. *Red* now dropped his work and waddled over to the group of organisms. There was a menacing brightness in the glow of his antenna knobs.

Green was right behind him. Bob and I watched the dramatic scene in motionless fascination.

Red seized a section which one of the attacking party had just brought back to its original position and deliberately reversed it once more. Meantime *Green* had laid his appendages on a second slab just being turned over by two other creatures and forced it down to the ground in its inverted position. A pitched battle ensued, a strange battle of swaying cubical forms and vibrating luminous antennae—a battle of tomblike silence.

As we watched in awe, a swarm of shell creatures suddenly appeared on the scene and joined the fracas. A milling, surging mob it was, with our two faithful friends in the centre of it, probably getting a sound drubbing for their trouble. Bob and I, the sole cause of this near riot, could do no more than stand helplessly on the sidelines, watching the considerably one-sided battle continue to its inevitable conclusion.

PRESENTLY the disturbance ceased and the crowd of shell people opened up. *Red* and *Green* were led forth, apparently none the worse for the punishment they had been receiving. It was plain to see however that they were now prisoners, as much under arrest as if they had been in irons. Waving a cheerful greeting to us, they were led off by most of the attacking party. The rest of the shell men remained behind to complete the restoration of the disturbed slabs.

Throughout the entire proceedings Bob and I had been completely ignored, just as though we had never existed. With the last portion of the surface back in its original state the shell creatures turned to us. They beckoned, and we obeyed mechanically. Strange to say we did not feel ourselves as being prisoners. There was no real indication of hostility about these enigmatic creatures. There was more a sense of hurt pride, of injured feelings, as though we had betrayed their trust, and they felt slightly annoyed in consequence.

Bob and I tramped along with our waddling escort. We exchanged only a word now and then. The first party with *Red* and *Green* in their midst was already out of sight. As we marched, I recognized some of the landmarks. We were being taken back to the ship. Presently, No. 43 hove into sight. Our faithful allies, with their escorting creatures, were nowhere in sight. Probably they had continued on to the city of the plain. I shuddered at the fate that might be in store for these two stouthearted little fellows. We reached the vessel, and our convoy of shell men stepped aside. Were we or were we not under arrest? Evidently not. Bob undid the door fastenings and we piled into our quarters once more.

We spent the day inside the ship, eating, resting, napping, protected from the blazing violence of the sun's rays. The dramatic battle of the night before and the probable fate of our two cubical allies was the chief topic of conversation. The next in importance was the question: What to do now? A startling fact made itself evident at this time. Inspection revealed that we had sufficient oxygen to last us only about three days. Signaling to Earth was now out of the question. If we were at all anxious to come out of this escapade alive, there was only one thing to do...to find immediate means to penetrate the shell with our vessel.

"We've got to dig a hole somewhere," I said seriously, "and get through...and in a hurry too, or we might as well write *finis* to the tale."

"But *dammitall!*" replied Bob. "How in thunder are we going to even begin to dig a hole? All we have to do is scratch the surface and..."

He was interrupted by a decidedly familiar rustling sound at the nearest window. Bob and I wheeled suddenly, to be confronted by…none other than our two faithful friends, *Red* and *Green.*

"They're out again!" called Bob gleefully.

And true enough they were…and none the worse for their hectic experience of the previous night. We had spent several mournful hours discussing the probable fate of these two intrepid shell men at the hands of their irate fellows…floggings…long imprisonment…perhaps capital punishment. Our hearts had gone out to the brave creatures in their last vain attempt to be of service to a couple of strange invaders from another world.

But here they were, as vigorous and healthy-looking as ever, waving their appendages joyously at the sight of us, acting as genuinely happy as though they had been human beings instead of organic cubes of color-speckled gelatine!

"Maybe they managed to escape," I ventured, "and sneak over to the ship."

"That's not very likely," replied Bob. He was at another window looking out upon the dimly lighted landscape, and pointed out to me at least eight other shell men visible here and there about the vicinity. "*Red* and *Green* are at large with the full knowledge of the rest of the people. Our little friends must have some considerable influence in the community to be able to talk their way out of *that* jam."

"And they seem to want us to come out again, don't they Bob?"

My friend agreed with me that they were apparently signaling us to join them outside. They certainly were gluttons for punishment!

We crawled into our space suits, and once more stood upon the dark surface of the shell. *Red* and *Green* cavorted about us gleefully.

"Wonder what they're up to now, Bob."

"That remains to be seen."

We strolled about aimlessly, with a watchful eye on our two friends, as well as on the other cubical beings visible nearby. Nothing much happened. *Red* and *Green* merely trailed along after us dutifully. The other native creatures paid no apparent attention to us. They went about their affairs as though there were no suspicions against either Bob and myself, or the pair of organisms that were dogging our footsteps. Completely forgotten it appeared was the recent battle of the ground slabs, as well as the deliberate desecration of the surface by these two traitorous shell beings. However, perhaps we had it all wrong. Maybe we misunderstood entirely the real significance of that vividly exciting spectacle of last night. Maybe ill had a completely different meaning, of which we were ignorant.

Most of the shell men had already sauntered out of sight. Only one or two were visible. *Red* and *Green* were still hovering dutifully behind us. There was a something about them of ominous expectancy that bespoke a promise of action in the very near future. Bob and I exchanged significant glances. And now the last of the shell creatures disappeared over the nearby ridge. We were alone with our two friends. They beckoned vigorously. We followed.

Off to the left we shot, and down into a shallow declivity, then over a slight rise and across a stretch of plain. It was our turn now to trail along after our rapidly moving allies. Luckily we encountered no other cubical beings...I say luckily, because Bob and I immediately surmised what was up. *Red* and *Green* were bent upon lending every ounce of their superhuman energy to the furtherance of our schemes. They knew that we had set our minds upon a certain plan of action. What the whole thing meant they probably were unable to fathom. But they were indomitable in their desire to see the accomplishment of our object, whatever it was. Right now, they knew that our chief aim was to reverse ground slabs. And reverse them they intended, or lose their lives in the attempt. Brave little chaps…

Reaching a locality with which they were evidently familiar, our guides stopped. They looked about carefully at first to see that we were entirely alone. Then *Red* beckoned us over to a spot and pointed to the ground. It showed evidences of having been disturbed. Many of the surface plates had been loosened and were ready to be turned over, although none of them had as yet been reversed.

"By George!" exclaimed Bob. "They've got it all prepared for us!"

"They refuse to stay licked," I added in admiration. "Their people stop them in one spot, and they pop right up somewhere else."

Red and *Green* stood by dutifully, as though awaiting further orders.

"But we can't go ahead with this signaling stunt, can we Bob?" I expostulated. "We've got to think of a quick getaway, rather than of sending a message."

"Right!" was my companion's terse reply, as though struck by a sudden inspiration. "And here's where we can start working on that very thing…a quick getaway!"

He was on his hands and knees in a jiffy, poring over the ground, laying out distances with outstretched arms, and acting in general in a very mystifying fashion. I watched him in bewilderment. The two shell men appeared to be equally puzzled at his unusual antics. Presently he rose to his feet.

"With the help of *Red* and *Green*," he announced, "we can excavate a passageway right here…a tunnel or shaft straight down into and through the shell, and large enough to permit the ship to pass through."

"How are you going to keep this whole operation secret?" I inquired.

"I've thought of that matter, Earl, and I believe I have the answer."

"And then how about the little matter of getting No 43 over to this spot?"

"I've already given some thought to that matter too, and it will be taken care of in due time. Say, can't you do anything except stand there and think up a lot of riddles? Come on, let's get to work!"

Bob turned over two slabs, each about four feet square, while I helped as best I could. This done, he beckoned to the two shell creatures. With appropriate gestures, he indicated that he wanted them to dig. They helped us willingly. Their luminary appendages zigzagged through the soft material beneath them. The stuff fairly sizzled into nothingness at the touch of those all-powerful bulbs. Bob and I had seen a similar performance back there at the spot, where the six rocketships were being dismantled, on the day we burst through the shell. But the speed and dispatch of the present demonstration made the other look like "slow motion." In less time than it takes to tell it, the indefatigable pair had excavated an oblong hole four feet deep. And as for the excavated debris…why it just vanished, turned into nothingness…perhaps converted into gases which were instantly dissipated into the vastness of empty space.

Bob sprang into the trench and directed the workers to apply their excavators laterally now, so as to burrow out below the adjacent surface layer. Our little helpers responded willingly. Soon they had hollowed out a chamber large enough for all of us to crawl into. They now gave their attention to the floor of the chamber, working away at that with deft sweeps of their powerful appendages. In moments, they had the cave deep enough and wide enough for Bob and me to stand up erect and move about with comparative comfort.

Red and *Green* appeared to comprehend the whole plan of things with almost miraculous intelligence. Before going any further in the excavating process, they fashioned a number of thin strips of ground substance, treating them in some mysterious fashion so as to render them rigid and strong. These they erected at various angles from the walls of the chamber to the roof, so as to support the surface slabs above us. The two sections that had been removed at the very start of the excavating operations they now carefully replaced, shoring them up in the same manner as the other portions of the roof. This accomplished, the two industrious cube creatures turned again to the job of digging. We must have made a grotesque picture there the four of us, hopping about the rapidly growing cave in the eerie pink illumination from the creatures' antennae, Bob and I making measurements and laying out dimensions. *Red* and *Green* working busily at the rubbery floors and walls, melting the stuff away, just as a hot sun melts away a snow bank, only with infinitely greater speed.

"Now here's the way I've figured the thing out," explained Bob as the work progressed. "We'll make the shaft about twenty feet wide...that is, *Red* and *Green* will...and roughly circular in shape. That will provide ample room for No. 43 to slip through, nose down when the time comes. We can dig our way down through the shell without any molestation from the rest of the shell people. I had an entirely different idea of how to keep the digging secret, but our good little friends here have worked out a scheme that has mine all beat. They've got the roof slabs securely shored up, and all evidences on the surface removed, so that even the keenest observers among their countrymen couldn't tell what's going on right beneath them. Why…there you are now…look!

Bob pointed up. The ceiling slabs were of course transparent and therefore invisible to us from below. The upper part of the shaft appeared as an extraordinarily wide circular opening, with the sky and the stars clearly visible. A form moved across the clear space above us, then another. I caught my breath. They were cube men, strolling leisurely over the top of the excavation. All unaware of the activity going on beneath the thin layer on which they moved, the shell beings passed on. From our position in the shaft, we could see them even after they had moved from directly overhead and continued to walk on more solid ground. Being on the *reverse side* of things, we were looking up at, and *right through* the adjacent ground over a wide area—looking through it as though it were so much clear plate glass. This explained why the twenty-foot circle had suddenly appeared to expand into one many times that size. The whole idea of the thing was so uncanny that I found it difficult to grasp the reality of it for some time. And not the strangest part of the entire proceedings was the utter indifference of *Red* and *Green* to things about and above them. Did they know of the curious semi-transparency of their shell substance? Were they conscious of the extraordinary spectacle visible over our heads? They gave no evidence of either knowing or caring. They merely bent to the task of annihilating the dark matter beneath them, and enlarging the cavity in conformity with the measurements laid out by Bob.

"Well, one thing is certain," I exclaimed in great relief, as the last of the shell people passed out of our range of vision above us. "We're safe from being bothered. They haven't the faintest suspicion about what's going on down here, and now for the rest of your plan, Bob."

"The big job, Earl, is to figure out how far down we ought to dig. To be sure, if we knew how thick the shell is, we could easily stop excavating at a point just short of the lower surface. As for the remaining obstruction, we would have to depend on the ship breaking through that thin layer on her own momentum. But, confound it all, there's no way of telling how thick or how thin the shell is. After all, it can't be very thick, because, when we burst through on our way up, there didn't seem to be more than a few seconds interval between the time we struck the underside and the time we landed on top."

"Of course," added Bob, "we could try this—if we tap on the ground with some hard object we ought to hear faint sound vibrations transmitted up through the feet and body to the ears. I've already tried a little of that, and it seems to work. As the thickness of material below us decreases, there should be a change in the sound produced. That ought to give us some measure of how much more we'd have to go to break through."

Bob and I turned our attention immediately to this task. With the butt end of his automatic, my companion tapped on the floor of the excavation. The soft ground sent back through our feet a faint response that was barely audible in our space helmets. Would there be any perceptible change in the nature of the vibrations as we approached bottom. Not a very reliable test, we admitted, but it was something…

Red and *Green* continued their machine-like excavating. We were now down to a depth of almost twenty feet. Employing no plumb lines or any other truing devices, these two remarkable workers had brought the walls down exactly perpendicular. Their precision was really extraordinary. As they progressed downward, they left a series of deep notches or steps in the wall to enable Bob and myself to ascend or descend with ease and safety. As for themselves, they needed no such artificial devices. They scampered freely up and down the vertical sides of the cave, aided by their thin hair-like appendages, as if they were a couple of enormous flies.

All through the night, the digging continued, and by the time, the sun rose for another day the shaft had been sunk to a depth of over thirty feet. We called a halt, and after making certain that no shell people were visible above us, we emerged through one of the removable slabs and stood again on solid ground. It was truly remarkable to see a smooth, unbroken expanse of dark surface, revealing not a trace of evidence to indicate the presence of a vast hole directly beneath.

Bob and I were extremely tired, as well as ravenously hungry. Our cubical assistants seemed to be as fresh and lively as though their monumental piece of work was merely child's play. They conducted us to our ship, passing *en route* several groups of shell men. Bob and I tried to look as unconcerned as possible. The creatures did not even give us a second glance. What unsuspecting and inordinately gullible beings! They had caught us red-handed on two different occasions, and here we were, out in public in the company of the perfidious *Red* and *Green*...and they merely observed us blankly and let us pass! Were they stung to action only by an obviously overt act? Were they fully aware of our machinations, and merely biding their time? It was impossible to determine what lay back of the imperturbable exterior of these enigmatic organisms.

Once at our vessel Bob arranged, through various signs and gestures to have our energetic little helpers meet us at the shaft at sundown. He had made particular note of routes, landmarks, etc, and was certain that we would find the spot again unassisted.

Shortly after noon, we were awakened by a disturbance outside. It was another meteor shower. The nearest of the speeding missiles fell at some distance from the ship, and was close enough to make us feel pretty uneasy. There were no shell creatures visible at the time, and it was difficult, from our position, to determine if any extensive damage had been done by the falling fragments.

However, sleep was no longer possible for either of us. We were worried no end about the safety of our partially excavated shaft. A direct hit would ruin our work and doom our chances of escape back to Earth. Even a less than direct hit would probably result in a dislodging of the surface plates covering the big hole and the exposure of our scheme. The mere thought of the ticklish situation, whichever way things eventuated, was sufficient to make both Bob and myself break into a cold sweat.

"We've got to hustle," said my companion. "This may be just a forerunner of what to expect from now on. Perhaps we are entering a period of increased meteor activity. If that's the case, we may see more and more of these fellows dropping down on us."

"And what's more, Bob," I added, "We have only about two days' supply of oxygen. There's no time to waste now."

Our situation was truly alarming from the point of view of both the meteor danger and the rapidly dwindling supply of the life-giving gas. Yet Bob was supremely confident that we would win the race against time and the elements.

Before sundown, we left the ship and made our way to the site of our excavation, hoping all the time that we would not arouse too much suspicion. None of the few shell beings whom we encountered along the way molested us, or even gave us much more than a casual glance. The spot was deserted, but we had waited hardly fifteen minutes when *Red* and *Green* hove into sight. We entered the shaft hurriedly, and the tireless workers plunged into the job with furious energy. They seemed to understand that time was precious—that every moment counted now. And they cut through that dark ground substance with a zeal that was truly astonishing. Bob and I were really superfluous—in fact far from being of any material assistance, we found ourselves very much in the way. *Red* and *Green* kept us hopping from one point in the huge hole to another as they tore away at the floor and walls. You could almost see the bottom of the shaft dropping away from under our feet.

FROM time to time, we tested out the vibrations transmitted up through our bodies in accordance with the scheme that Bob had developed. We tapped away dutifully upon the soft ground, and listened for any change in the nature of the tone that resulted. To be perfectly frank, I was unable to detect any greatly marked differences at different levels. There might have been some change in pitch, in fact, I could swear that the sound did appear to alter slightly, but the conditions of the test were so uncertain as to make the results extremely unreliable. Bob was finally forced to admit that we could not place much faith in the tests. We'd just have to trust to luck. It was simply a case of stabbing in the dark. At some point, and that very soon, we must call a halt on the digging operation.

By sunrise, the shaft was nearly eighty feet deep. Bob and I now put our heads together. Should we continue? If we were suddenly to "hole through," then what? Why nothing more serious than a nice little tumble for the four of us...a tumble of over 130 miles to solid ground...a breath-taking stunt, even the mere thought of it made me gasp.

We decided to call the job finished right here and now. The hole was deep enough. A few feet more or less would hardly make any material difference. Back in No. 43 only a single day's supply of oxygen remained! Moreover, ominous rumblings had been coming to us all through the night at longer or shorter intervals. They denoted but one thing—the meteors were becoming more numerous. Most of the vibrations, to be sure, were faint, indicating that the flying fragments were striking at comfortably great distances from us. Nevertheless, the idea was not really a pleasant one to contemplate. How could we be sure that at the very next instant a huge mass of matter wouldn't decide to come down right on our diggings, and wipe us out in one fell swoop, or what was equally possible, strike our ship and leave us stranded high and dry?

Bob and I hastily clambered to the surface, with our gelatinous helpers right at our heels. They replaced the trapdoor slab and turned to us for further orders. Bob motioned them to come and we set off in the direction of the ship. We reached it in record time. Sleep was out of the question now. Minutes were precious. Low mutterings came vibrating through the ground and up into our bodies. Meteors were falling with increasing frequency. Their sinister rumblings made my very soul tremble. We couldn't wait until the next sundown to stage our escape. It had to be done right now...

Our innermost hopes and forebodings appeared to pass like a contagion to the consciousness of *Red* and *Green*. Evidently they sensed the air of apprehension—the unusual tension of things—the importance of haste. And as for the rest of the cubical creatures, they also seemed aware that there was something "in the wind." Engrossed as they were with the alarming matter of the falling meteors, they showed signs that our sudden haste was not going without notice.

"Just a last test on the rockets," I said briefly when we reached the ship.

"And then we can move!" was Bob's terse reply.

I struggled with the door lock for a few moments. The mechanism was still erratic in its operation. Having been somewhat dislocated at the time we burst through the shell, it had given trouble nearly every time we had occasion to open or close it in our frequent goings and comings. Several times Bob had attempted to repair it, without success.

Well, there was no time to think of such trifles now. I finally managed to open the trap and proceeded into the interior of the ship, while Bob waited outside. Without even removing my spacesuit I busied myself with the controls.

"Inside!" I called loudly into my helmet transmitter. "I'm going to test out unit Number 43 for a minute, Bob. Watch out!"

"Let her rip!" came Bob's cheery voice in my earpieces. I opened the fuel valves and applied the switch. A slight quiver ran through the vessel. After about ten seconds of firing, I shut off the unit.

"Works fine!" was Bob's grim comment as I emerged through the outer hatch. "And the folks here are all excited about it too! Just look at them!" Shell men seemed to spring right out of nowhere and come flocking to the spot. For the time being, they seemed to have forgotten the menace of the meteors. Again, they appeared to consider themselves as witnesses of a scientific demonstration, similar to the others to which we had treated them. Their motions and gestures sent a message that was as plain as day...they wanted more! *Red* and *Green*, in the front rank of the spectators, were equally vociferous with the rest…that is vociferous in the manner of their type of speechless communication.

"Try one or two of the lateral units, Earl," said Bob. "But for Heaven's sake, only a couple of seconds firing at the most! We haven't any fuel to waste!"

Again, I darted into the chamber.

Two of the side rockets responded to my touch and then ceased promptly as I switched off the controls. I joined Bob outside. "Everything's ready," I whispered.

A rush of meteors at some distance from us threw the assembled crowd into a little bit of a panic. The shower halted momentarily, and the disturbed multitude calmed down.

Bob motioned to *Red* and *Green*. They responded as though they were trained seals. Bob's gestures indicated that he wanted the vessel lifted. The two cubical creatures sent a flashing communication to their fellowmen. Evidently, our two friends still had plenty of influence with their brethren of the shell world, in spite of the little difficulty which had transpired several days ago.

Two score or more of the cubical organisms closed in upon the ship. Applying their power appendages to various portions of the metallic surface, they heaved in unison. The massive bulk was lifted bodily off the ground. We led the way, with strangely perambulating No 43 following along majestically. Those shell creatures who could not crowd around the ship and lend their immediate support scampered vivaciously about the moving mass, or else followed along behind, forming a straggling tail to the unusual procession.

"I wonder what they think we're up to," I whispered to my companion.

"Maybe they have an idea we're out to give them a bigger and better demonstration."

"As indeed we really *are!*" I added grimly.

"Perhaps they are under the impression, Earl, that we're scared of the meteors, and so we're merely moving the ship to some other location where we believe it will be safer."

"Well, they can believe anything they please, Bob, as long as they don't guess the truth."

"They'll soon learn that all right."

"It seems strange, doesn't it, that they're so willing and eager to be of service to us, after that rumpus they kicked up with us about moving those ground slabs?"

"It appears to me, Earl, that that's their pet aversion. Any time they catch us monkeying with their precious ground, that's the time we may expect trouble. But so long as we keep our hands off, then they are the sweetest, boniest sort of creatures. Isn't that the size of it?"

"That explains it all, Bob. Right now, they're the greatest help imaginable. But, oh boy! If they only knew..."

"They're going to know...pretty soon..."

As we trudged along with the great mob behind us, Bob outlined his scheme for the take-off. His idea was to have the vessel brought to the edge of the concealed shaft, and so placed that her nose would extend out a few feet over the excavated portion. Then, by suitable props placed under her middle and her tail, she would be given a tilt forward and downward. When all was ready, we would hop in and "give her the gun," so to speak, firing several units from the rear, as well as a number of the lateral rockets. The unequal thrust would be sufficient to force the nose of the ship down with considerable violence on the thin roof structure of the shaft. The rest would be easy...a drop straight down the eighty foot shaft to the floor...a bursting through the remaining thickness of shell material (a thickness of indeterminate extent, by the way!)...and then a sheer drop of 130 miles, controlled of course by the decelerating effect of the braking rockets in the ship's nose...concluded by a graceful landing on Mother Earth!

HOW thrilling the whole idea sounded! And yet how fraught with danger! How many uncertain factors there were in the entire scheme! Suppose the shell men discovered our duplicity before we could make our escape...suppose the ship refused to drop accurately into the prepared hole in the ground...suppose the unexcavated portion would prove too thick for even the tremendous momentum of No. 43 to effect a breaking through, and we remained stuck fast like a bullet in a trunk *(Dammit!* Why hadn't we gone down 150 feet...200 feet...even more, instead of a paltry 80? But there was the time element! And our dwindling oxygen supply!) Suppose we did "hole through" successfully and then ran short of fuel? Whew, what an idea! No possibility of braking in that furious descent...a drop through the atmosphere like an incandescent torch! To strike the Earth as a mess of gorgeous cinders!

And so we tramped along in the van of this strange parade, going over each phase of the plan in subdued whispers. Unconsciously our tones were hushed and tense, although we could just as well have shouted our schemes to the very sky and still enjoy perfect secrecy. The shell men swept along behind us in holiday mood—as though this were one great lark.

Red and *Green* were of course right there beside us all the time. And what of these two brave fellows? Could we now, on the very eve of our dramatic departure, convey to them adequately our deep gratitude for the well nigh indispensable aid which they had rendered us? And what was the motivating factor in their boundless devotion to us? Would we ever know?

Now we had arrived at the very site itself. The surface presented a smooth and almost untouched appearance. But this was the spot, all right. Certain, definite characteristics served to stamp it indelibly in our minds. We estimated the outline of the shaft by several almost insignificant markings. The shell men halted with their burden, as though waiting for orders to place the ship at some designated point. Bob motioned and the vessel was maneuvered around deftly. Again, a signal from Bob and Number 43 was gently lowered. He now motioned to *Red* and *Green.* A few appropriate gestures and they understood. Would the rest of the shell populace countenance the next move? It remained to be seen. Our two assistants cut several long strips of ground material and treated them with that mysterious ray or emanation from their lighted appendages, as they had done once before in the shaft. The strips became rigid as steel bars. There was an uneasy stirring among the ranks of the cube people, but they did not molest the two at their work. Evidently they were satisfied that this procedure was essential to the success of the forthcoming demonstration—as long as there was no attempt to dislodge ground slabs and reverse them as on that other memorable occasion.

Our helpers now entered into communication with their countrymen. Presently a squad of them laid hold of the ship and slowly raised the tail off the surface. *Red* and *Green* quickly slipped the rigid ground strips under the elevated portion. They then hastened to prepare several rods that are more similar and inserted them into place. Bob waved his satisfaction and thanks. The shell men stepped back. No. 43 was now ready…

During the course of the preparations, Bob and I voiced considerable apprehension to each other. The cubical creatures were swarming all about the place, a good many of them crowding over the roof portion of the hidden shaft. Would it hold? What if the flimsy shoring should give way and the thin layer of ground slabs collapse under the weight of the multitude? But the roof held. Either it was the extreme lightness of the shell people, or else the seemingly frail supports were far stronger than we had suspected—and sufficiently rigid to hold up the great crowd that surged on the surface slabs.

Well, we were ready to go. The area over the shaft would first have to be cleared. There was no sense in causing any greater casualties to the shell people than we had to. It pained us deeply to realize that our precipitous departure would necessarily do some damage among those creatures that happened to be closest to us. That was inevitable. Yet we could minimize the extent of the catastrophe, if we shooed them away to a respectable distance. Bob started out from where the rocketship was poised and strode across the top of the shaft, waving back the hoard of cube creatures. *Red* and *Green* were with him, helping to sweep the rest of the shell people from the area directly over the excavation. As for myself, I circled the ship and did likewise to the crowds that pressed about it. I succeeded in getting them back a dozen feet or so. They offered no resistance, seemingly certain that the stage was being set for a grand show. And it truly was.

Coming back to the nose of the ship, close to the hatch, I perceived that Bob together with his team of helpers had succeeded fairly well. Most of the crowd had been persuaded to move away from the imaginary circle that denoted the excavation. A few stragglers were still waddling about in the danger area. Bob was now well beyond the far side of the circle, about fifty feet from where I stood. He turned and looked back across the partially cleared area to where the ship lay tilted.

Suddenly a dark streak shot through space. Instant pandemonium broke loose over to the left on the fringe of the crowd of cube beings. A meteor! Several more came hurtling down and crashed some distance away. I could feel the ground tremble beneath my feet. The terrified creatures broke into motion. Some of them began to close in on the cleared area. Others at the outskirts of the multitude commenced to disperse in all directions.

I yelled across to Bob, although what it was that I called to him, I am not sure. He started toward me. He took but one step when it happened…

A dark smear stabbed downward between us. The hurtling meteor—a relatively tiny fragment—struck the roof of the shaft and disappeared below, leaving a jagged, yawning hole about six feet in diameter. And along with it there disappeared also two or three unfortunate cube men that happened to be moving about at that spot.

For a moment the crowd of creatures was taken aback by the startling suddenness of this new revelation. Other meteors fell nearby, but they were completely ignored. Awakened suddenly to action, the nearest of the shell men hastened to the edge of the gaping hole. Others began crowding about it. All danger was forgotten. They were intent on only one thing—this sudden and amazing manifestation…

""THE jig's up!" came Bob's startled words loudly into my earpieces. "They're on to us for fair…no telling what they'll do now. We've got to get away from here this *very minute!*"

He lunged forward through the crushing mass of shell creatures, making a wide detour so as to circle around the outside of the roof area. I could see him fighting his way inch by inch. It was only a few feet, yet it must have seemed like miles to him. And now he was by my side.

For a fleeting moment I had been rooted to the spot by the sheer drama of the situation. Now I was galvanized into action. We both turned to the ship. Two leaps brought us to the door. Confound that infernal lock! *Jammed once more!* And at the most crucial moment too! We tugged...and swore out loud. It refused to budge. I shot a hasty glance over my shoulder. The mob of shell people that had cleared away from the immediate vicinity of the ship was now closing in, their mien one of unmistakable menace. Over on the circle, with its dark hole in the centre, the crowd milled and surged. Some of them were making toward the ship too.

From overhead the rain of destruction was coming down with increasing fury. Large and small meteors were falling with increasing frequency. The destruction among the shell people was appalling. Yet they seemed to pay scant heed to the fury from above. They were being consumed by a fury of their own. We Earth men had dared to commit the unpardonable sin—had dared to molest their sacred surface covering—to dig down through their shell substance with secrecy and duplicity. And such treachery would not go unavenged...

Madly Bob and I tugged at the door. It suddenly gave, and swung outward. As it did so, I felt a strange pull at my elbow. We turned and looked. There were *Red* and *Green.* They had followed Bob through the milling throng. And their mute appeal was as real and as vivid as a spoken message.

"Well, I'll be!" blurted Bob.

"They want to come along!"

"No harm!" I shouted back. "Let's take 'em...*as souvenirs!*"

I clambered into the doorway as Bob gave me a terrific heave to hasten my progress. Once in, I reached back to drag him in behind me. Following him came the faithful pair of helpers who refused to be left behind.

The multitude of shell men were shocked into momentary inactivity by this sudden turn of events. What was the meaning of *this?* Two shell men deserting their fellows and casting their lot with the invaders from another world!

With glowing antennae waving a threat of vengeance and retribution, the creatures flung themselves from all directions upon the ship.

"To blazes with the air lock!" shouted Bob hoarsely.

I then abandoned the attempt to fasten the inner door device and hurled myself at the controls. On went tail units No. 1, 2 and 4...lateral units No. 6 and 8! The ship was quivering in every joint. She heaved over sharply, nose down, stern flung straight up into space. Bob and I held on tightly to whatever supports were available. I could see *Red* and *Green* huddled together over in a corner of the control chamber.

One...two seconds of headlong fall! I jammed shut the fuel feeds to laterals 6 and 8. The stern units blazed away furiously.

Crash! The ship shook until I thought she would fly to pieces. A grinding and a sloshing...that familiar sensation we had experienced once before on our up-trip. No. 43 was tearing through the solid shell material. Would we go all the way through? Would we jam to a fearful stop before reaching the lower surface?

Then, another noticeable quiver! The grinding noise had ceased...our speed was picking back up! *The skip had holed through!* We were shooting back toward Earth at an ultra-fast pace.

With a loud cry of exultation, I swung the lever that throttled the stern units and applied the braking rockets in the nose. Our speed gradually decreased. Bob stood at the window opposite the control panel gazing fixedly out toward the stern of the ship. I followed his gaze to see a deeply violet sky, with myriad pinpoints of light flecking its vast expanse. The yellow orb of the sun shone forth in the midst of it all.

"And we're looking right through it, too," he muttered, "right through that mysterious shell of one-way transparency."

A number of dark masses whizzed past our ship and hurtled down toward the Earth. One or two came perilously close. They seemed almost to brush the sides of No. 43 in their swift flight. Since our rate of drop had been materially slowed up by the decelerating influence of the nose rockets, we appeared almost to be standing still in comparison.

"The meteors are still falling thick and fast up there," I remarked with an upward gesture of my hand, "and breaking right through the shell."

"This is a *real* shower," commented Bob gravely, as the missies flew by in increasing numbers. "Just imagine the havoc they're doing to those creatures up on the shell. Poor wretches…"

I slowed up our rate of descent. Bob and I prayed inwardly that we escape the wrath of the oncoming meteoric storm, just as we had so miraculously weathered the others on the shell surface. Apparently it was the decision of a kindly fate that we were to be spared. The shower soon abated. All was now serene throughout. The ship continued its smooth descent and we began to breathe a bit more more easily.

Over in the corner *Red* and *Green* were still in their original positions. Overwhelmed by the kaleidoscopic succession of events, bewildered by the inordinate strangeness of new surroundings and new experiences, they could do no more than stare (or the cubical equivalent of stare). Bob waved a cheerful greeting to them, and they responded feebly.

AFTER the first few tense minutes in our new situation, I suddenly became aware of an unusual circumstance. I burst into a shout of laughter.

"Why, Bob," I cried, "do you realize that we're still wearing these space togs—helmets and all? And right here inside the ship, too! That's what I call rich!"

"Darned if I didn't clean forget about it," replied Bob in huge amusement. "Things were happening so fast, it just didn't enter my mind."

He suddenly moved to the instrument panel and consulted it. Then a soft exclamation sounded in my helmet phones. He jumped across the chamber to the air lock.

"It's a mighty lucky thing we kept these outfits on," he called out. "Just take a slant at that pressure indicator, Earl…"

I glanced curiously at the instrument, and uttered a muffled cry. I peered at my wrist recorder to compare the reading.

Both devices registered a pressure of *zero millimeters—a perfect vacuum!*

"It's this infernal air lock again," explained Bob as he worked at the mechanism. "In our haste about getting aboard we didn't fasten the catch properly—you know it's been out of kilter ever since we landed on the shell. Well, the air has all escaped—probably disappeared in a few seconds after we opened the doors."

"And if we had ripped off our space suits at the very start then… Whew what a close one that was…"

"I'll have this door sealed up tight in a jiffy," announced Bob, "then we can boost up the pressure inside and be comfortable once more. How's the oxygen supply holding up?"

I consulted the meter on the last reserve tank. "Not much left," I replied, "but I think there's enough to last us until we get back to Earth."

Our cubical passengers were still in their corner, watching the proceedings with evident interest. Bob continued to work on the door device, while I stood at the controls. Presently a low cry of satisfaction from Bob announced that the job was finished.

"That'll hold nicely until we land," he said. He came over to my side of the ship and opened the valves to build up the artificial atmosphere within the chamber. The barometric needle swung steadily about the dial. In less than a minute the air in the room was at normal pressure. Bob hurriedly discarded his cumbersome suit and helmet and flung them far from himself, as though happy to get rid of them—and well he might be! Then he took over the ship's controls for a few moments while I likewise divested myself of the *impediments.*

Suddenly my companion burst forth with a cry of anguish—of genuine heart-tearing anguish.

"Look! For pity's sake..." he pointed to the far corner. I wheeled in astonishment to follow his gaze. My blood nearly froze in my veins at the spectacle.

Red and *Green* were...well...they were *no more.*

In their place were two almost completely flattened colored masses—just cozy smears on the floor. I was across the room in a flash. Bob abandoned the controls and was by my side. We gazed in complete horror at the awful sight. The realization of the terrible tragedy dawned upon us almost simultaneously.

The pressure was incredible! Nearly fifteen pounds to the square inch! These poor creatures had been created to live only in a total vacuum...the crushing weight of the artificial atmosphere within the ship had literally squashed their frail bodies...had flattened out the porous cubes just as though a tremendous roller had passed over them. We knelt beside the mortal remains of our loyal little friends from a strange world. The twisted appendages that lay sprawled out on the floor still exuded a pale glow at the knobbed ends, although that light was failing rapidly even as we looked. It seemed to me that one of the luminous antennae was twitching nervously. I called Bob's attention to it. He agreed that the appendage was moving faintly. Was it a last feeble gesture from those redoubtable creatures? Was it a final farewell wave before their souls were wafted to a distant Valhalla of shell people? We looked somberly at each other and let it go at that...

Sadly, Bob and I returned to our tasks. There was an ache in our hearts that could not easily be dispelled. Silently we guided the ship back on her course toward solid Earth. We entered the denser layers of the atmosphere, and the violet aspect of the space about as slowly turned into familiar daylight. I checked the ship's descent, and, when about fifteen miles from the surface, we took our bearings. We found ourselves over the region of the Great Lakes. In a few moments, the ship's nose was pointing southeast, and we were executing a graceful curved descent that would land us in New York.

Almost unnoticed the flyer dropped to a smooth landing on the Stratosphere Transport field. Had we completed our mission?

Mission? What mission?

Oh, yes, to be sure, those lost rocketships. We had located them. And we had discovered a new world, an invisible world, and yet a very material one. And we had brought back two flattened heaps of red and green gelatin as evidences of the life that existed up there in that dim shell-world "beyond the stratosphere."

THE END

ENTER THE FOREST OF DEATH AT YOUR OWN RISK!

Lost in the depth of the hell-forest of Ganymede was a secret ancient race whose weird technologies and knowledge were Earth's only chance of survival against a plague ravaging mankind. But to retrieve this knowledge, a staunch group of soldiers would have to battle vampiric carnivorous plants, poisonous butterflies (whose larvae could eat a man alive), and the hypnotic spores of the Noctoli flower, from which no man could escape. In addition, there were even worse terrors lying in wait within the dreaded Black Forest. But if any man could lead this group through the vile depths of the forest to the sinister fortress of the Ancient Ones, it would be Ed Garth. Garth had once before defied the odds and escaped the clutches of the hell-forest's most fearsome beasts, but could he do it again, especially now with Earth's very survival weighing upon his shoulders?

AUTHOR PORTRAIT

Henry Kuttner, 1915-1958

CRYPT-CITY OF THE DEATHLESS ONE

By
HENRY KUTTNER

ARMCHAIR FICTION
PO Box 4369, Medford, Oregon 97504

The original text of this novel was first published by Love Romances Publishing Co.

For more information about Armchair Books and products, visit our website at…

www.armchairfiction.com

Or email us at…

armchairfiction@yahoo.com

CHAPTER ONE

ICY WATER splashed into Ed Garth's face and dripped down his tattered, grimy shirt. It was a tremendous effort to open his eyes. Fumes of the native Ganymedean rotgut liquor were swimming in his brain.

Someone was shaking him roughly. Garth's stocky body jerked convulsively. He struck out, his drink-swollen face twisted with frightened fury, and gasped, *"Ylgana! Vo m'trana al-khron—"*

The hand on his shoulder fell away.

Someone said, "That's it, Paula! The Ancient Tongue!"

And a girl's voice, doubtful, a little disgusted.

"You're sure? But how in the System did this—this—"

"Bum. Tramp," Garth muttered, peering blearily at the pale ovals of unfocused faces above him. "Don't mind me, sister. Beachcomber is the word—drunk, right now. So please get the hell out and let me finish my bottle."

More water was sluiced on Garth. He shook his head, groaning, and saw Tolomo, the Ganymedean trader, scowling down at him. The native's three-pupiled eyes were angry.

English hissed, oddly accented, on his tongue.

"You wake up, Garth! Hear me? This is a job for you. You owe me too much already. These people come looking for you, say they want a guide. Now you do what they want, and pay me for all that liquor you buy on credit."

"Sure," Garth said wearily. "Tomorrow. Not now."

Tolomo snorted. "I get you native guides. Captain Brown. They know way to Chahnn."

The man's voice said stubbornly, "I don't want natives. I want Ed Garth."

"Well, you won't get him," Garth growled, pillowing his head on his arms. "This joint smells already, but you make it worse. Beat it."

CRYPT-CITY OF THE DEATHLESS ONE

By Henry Kuttner

He did not see Captain Brown slip Tolomo a folded credit-current. The trader deftly pocketed the money, nodded,

Only once could a man defy the deathless guardians of the Ancient's tomb-city deep in Ganymede's hell-forest and expect to live. Yet Ed Garth had to return, had to lead men to certain doom—to keep a promise to a girl he would never see again.

and gripped Garth by the hair, lifting his head. The bluish, inhuman face was thrust into the Earthman's.

"Listen to me, Garth," Tolomo said, fairly spitting the words. "I let you come in here and get drunk all the time on the cuff. You pay me a little, not much, whenever you gather enough alka-roots to sell. But you owe plenty. People ask me why I should let a bum like you come to my *Moonflower-Ritz Bar—* "

"That's a laugh," Garth mouthed. "A ramshackle plastic flophouse full of cockroaches and bad liquor. *Moonflower-Ritz*, hogwash!"

"Shut up," Tolomo snapped. "I let you run up a bill here when nobody else would. Now you take this job and pay me or I have the marshal put you in jail. At hard labor, in the swamps."

Garth called Tolomo something unprintable. "Okay," he groaned. "You win, louse. You know damn well no Earthman can stand swamp work, even with bog-shoes. Now let go of my hair before I smash your teeth in."

"'You do it? You guide these people?"

"I said I would, didn't I?" Garth reached fumblingly for the bottle before him. Someone thrust a filled glass into his hand. He gulped the fiery purplish liquor, shuddered, and blew out his breath.

"Okay," he said. "Welcome to Ganymede, the pleasure spot of the System. The worst climate outside Hell, the only world almost completely unexplored, and the nicest place for going to the dogs I've ever seen. The Chamber of Commerce greets you. Here's the representative." He pointed to a six-legged lizard with the face of a gargoyle that scuttled over the table and leaped into the shadows where the light of the radio-lamp did not reach.

Captain Brown said, "I can offer you fifty dollars to guide us to the ruined city—Chahnn. And, maybe, I can offer you *ten thousand bucks* to do another little job for us."

THE SHOCK of that was more effective than cold water had been. Garth jerked back, for the first time looking at his companions. There were two of them—a man and a girl, their neat tropical outfits looking out of a place in this grimy dive. The man was thin and bronzed, looking as though all the moisture had been boiled out of him by hot suns. He was made of tough leather, Garth thought. His face was the most expressionless one Garth had ever seen—pale, shallow eyes, a rat-trap mouth, and the general air of a tiger taking it easy.

The girl…sudden sick pain struck through Garth. She looked like Moira. For an incredible moment he thought, with his liquor-dulled mind, that she had come back. But Moira was dead—had been, for nearly five years now.

Five years of living death—hitting the skids on Ganymede, where men go down fast. Garth's ravaged face hardened. He forced himself to look squarely at the girl.

She wasn't Moira, after all. She had the same look of sleek, clean femininity, but her hair was golden-red instead of brown, and her eyes were greenish, not blue. The softness in her face was belied by the stubborn, rounded chin.

"Ten thousand?" Garth repeated softly. "I don't get the picture. Any native could take you to Chahnn."

The girl said, "We know that. We're interested in—something else. Could you use ten grand?"

"Yeah! Yeah, I could," Garth said.

"What would you do with it? Go back to Earth? We might swing it so you could get a job there. There's been a shortage of men ever since the Silver Plague started."

Garth laid his fingers gently around the glass and squeezed, till the transparent plastic was bent out of shape. He didn't look at the girl.

"I'm through with Earth. If I could collect—ten thousand?—I'd commit suicide, in a very funny way. I'd go into the Black Forest. The money could get me the men and equipment I'd need, but—well, nobody gets out of the Black Forest alive."

"You did," Captain Brown said.

"Eh? You heard about that?"

"We've heard stories—plenty of them. About how you came out of the Black Forest six years ago, raving with fever and talking in a language nobody could understand. And how you've been taking trips into the Forest ever since. Just what happened? I know you tried to get up expeditions to rescue a man named Willard—he was with you, wasn't he?"

Garth felt again that sick deadness in his brain—the monstrous question that had been tormenting him for five years now. Abruptly he slammed his fist on the table. Tolomo's face appeared behind a curtain and vanished again as Brown waved him back.

"Forget it," Garth said. "Even on Ganymede, men mind their own business—usually."

Brown stroked his cheek with a calloused thumb. "Suit yourself. Here's the set-up, then. It's strictly confidential, or the deal's off. You'll know why later. Anyhow—we want you to guide us into the Black Forest."

GARTH'S laughter rang harsh and bitter. Brown and the girl watched him with impassive eyes.

"What's so funny about it?" she asked, scowling.

Garth sobered. "Nothing much. Only for five years I've been sweating blood trying to get into the Forest, and I know the place better than anybody on Ganymede. See this?" He rolled up his sleeve and exhibited a purplish scar along his arm. "A cannibal-plant did that. I couldn't get away from the thing. Bullets and knives don't hurt the bloodsucker. I had to stand there for two hours, helpless, till it got all the blood it wanted. After that I managed to pull away."

"I've picked up a few scars myself," Brown said quietly.

Garth glared at him. "Not in the Black Forest. The only way to get through that pesthole is with a big, armed expedition. Even then...you ever heard of the Noctoli?"

"No. Who—"

"Flowers. Their pollen works funny—plenty funny. They grow in the interior, and they give you amnesia. Not even gasmasks help. The stuff works in through your skin."

"Doesn't it affect you?" the girl wanted to know.

Garth shivered and drank again. "It did—once. Later I managed to work out an antitoxin. And I've built up immunity, anyway. But it's quite a laugh. The two of you wanting to go into the Black Forest!"

Brown's face was emotionless. "With an expedition, well armed. I'll provide that."

"Oh. That's a bit different. Just the same—what are you after?"

"Just sightseeing," the girl said.

Garth grinned crookedly. "Okay. I know the stories. Everybody on Ganymede's heard of the *Ancients.*"

Captain Brown's eyes hooded. "What about them?"

"The lost race? That they lived on Ganymede thousands of years ago, and had the greatest science ever known to the System. That they died, nobody knows how, and the secrets of their civilization were lost. Chahnn's only one of their ruined cities. There've been a dozen others found. And full of gadgets and robots that nobody knows how to work. There was a central power-source, but Earthmen have never figured out how it worked or what fuel was used. The inscriptions found in the cities didn't tell anything."

"Fair enough," Brown nodded. "Except you forgot one thing. You know the Ancient Tongue. You speak it."

Garth chewed his lip. "So what?"

"Where did you learn it?"

"I don't know. In the Black Forest, I suppose. I don't remember."

The girl made an impatient gesture. She quieted as Brown glanced at her.

"From the Zarno, Garth?"

"I don't know! There's no proof the Zarno even exist!"

"If you've gone far enough into the Black Forest—"

Garth said angrily, "Remember what I told you about the Noctoli? The effect of the pollen? When I got back to Oreport here I had amnesia. I—" He hesitated. "I don't remember. I never did remember what happened in the Black Forest."

"Um-m." Brown rubbed his cheek again. "A lost race of savages no outsiders have ever seen—a race speaking the tongue of the Ancients. How could they live around those Noctoli flowers of yours?"

"Natural immunity," Garth said. "Built up over a period of generations. I didn't have that—then."

THE GIRL leaned forward, ignoring Brown. "Mr. Garth," she said swiftly, "I think I'd better explain a bit more. Shut up, Carver!" She frowned at Brown. "There've been too many mysteries. Here's the set-up. I've got half of a—a map. It shows the location of something in the Black Forest that's immensely valuable—the greatest treasure the System's ever known. I don't know what it is. The original inscription, in the Ancient's language, is cryptic as the devil. But the Ancients thought this treasure important enough to be worth hiding in the Black Forest. They set the Zarno to guard it. See?"

Garth grunted. "So what?"

"Well—I'm Paula Trent, archaeologist. Not that it matters. For months Carver and I have been waiting our chance to fit out an expedition and come on here. We didn't have the money, at first, and when we did get it, the government refused us permission. We had no proof, they said, and the Black Forest is impenetrable. So we waited. A month ago we got wind of a research ship, the *Hunter*, coming on here to investigate Chahnn. The same old stuff—digging around in the ruins, trying to find out what made the machines and robots tick, trying to make sense out of the inscriptions. Trying to find a cure for the Silver Plague."

Garth said, "No cure's been found yet, then."

Paula shook her head. "No. Since it started on Earth ten years ago, it's wiped out one-twentieth of the population, and unless it's stopped, it'll destroy all life on our world. But that's old stuff. Except the government's sending out their best men to Ganymede, because it's known the Silver Plague existed here once and was conquered. The inscriptions in Chahnn show that. But they don't say what the treatment was, or give any hints. However—" She brushed red-gold hair from her forehead. "Carver and I have planted men in the *Hunter* crew. Tough, good men who'll strike out with us into the Black Forest. With equipment."

"Desertion, eh?"

"Technically, sure. But the only way. Nobody will listen to us. We know—we know—the Ancients hid their most valuable treasure in the Black Forest. What it is we don't know. We're hoping it'll solve a lot of problems—the mystery of what powered their machines, what happened to the Ancients—all that."

"No planes can be used," Garth said. "There's no place to land in the Forest."

"That's why we want you. You know the Forest, and you know the Ancient Tongue. Guide the *Hunter* crew to Chahnn. Then, when we give the word—head for the Black Forest with us."

Garth said, "On one condition. You can't go."

Paula's eyes narrowed. "You're in no position to—"

"Men might get through. A woman couldn't. Take it or leave it," Garth repeated stubbornly.

Captain Brown nodded to the girl. "All right, it's a deal. Sorry, Paula, but he's on the beam. Here's ten bucks, Garth. Balance when we get to Chahnn. We leave tomorrow at Jupiter-rise."

GARTH didn't answer. After a moment Paula and Brown rose and went out through the mildewed tapestry curtain. Garth didn't blame them. The *Moonflower-Ritz* smelled.

Presently he found Tolomo and gave him the money. The Ganymedean hissed worriedly.

"Only ten?"

"You'll get the rest later. Gimme a bottle."

"I don't think—"

Garth reached across the bar and seized a quart. "Hereafter I do my drinking out-of-doors," he remarked. "I'll feel cleaner."

"Sfant!" Tolomo flung after him as he headed for the door. Garth's cheeks burned red at the word, which is Ganymedean and untranslatable; but he didn't turn. He stepped out into the muddy street, a cold wind, sulphurous and strong, stinging his nostrils.

He looked around at the collection of plastic native huts. Till the *Hunter* had arrived, he'd been the only Earthman in Oretown. Now—

He didn't feel like talking to natives. The Tor towered against the purple sky, where three of Jupiter's moons were glowing lanterns. At the base of the Tor was Garth's shack.

Swaying a little, clutching the bottle, he headed in that direction. He had waited five years for this moment. Now, when at last he might find the answer to the problem that had turned him into a derelict, he was afraid.

He went into his hut, switched on the radiolite, and stood staring at a door he had not opened for a long time. With a little sigh he pushed at the latch. The smell of musty rot drifted out.

A lamp revealed a complete medical laboratory, one that had not, apparently, been used for months at least. Garth almost dropped a bottle as he fumbled it from the shelf. Cursing, he opened the rotgut Ganymedean whiskey and poured it down his throat.

That helped. Steadied somewhat, he went to work. The Noctoli pollen antitoxin was still here, but it might have lost its efficacy.

He tested it.

Good. It seemed strong, the antibodies having a long life cycle. It would work.

Garth packed a compact medical kit. After that he stood for quite a while staring at two blank spaces on the wall, where pictures had once hung.

Moira and Doc Willard.

Damn! Garth snatched up the liquor and fled the house. He fought his way along the steep path that led to the Tor's summit. The physical exertion was a relief.

AT THE TOP, he sat down, his back against a rock. Beneath him lay Oretown, yellow-blue lights winking dimly. In a cleared field some distance away was the ovoid shape of the spaceship that had brought Paula and Brown—the *Hunter*. To the west, across sandy desert, lay Chahnn, dead city that had once housed an incredibly advanced science—lost now, its people dust. Northwest, beyond distant ridges, was the Black Forest, unexplored, secret, menacing.

Six years ago Dr. Jem Willard had come to Ganymede with his intern, Ed Garth. Willard was trying to discover the cure for the Silver Plague that was wrecking Earth. He would have found it—he had got on the track. But—

An emergency call had come in one night. A native needed an appendectomy. Willard couldn't fly a plane. He had called on Garth, and Garth had been drunk.

But he had piloted the plane anyhow. The crack-up happened over the Black Forest.

That was the last thing Garth remembered, or almost the last. It would have been more merciful if the oblivion had been complete. Months later he staggered out of the Forest into Oretown, alone. The Noctoli poison had almost erased his experiences from his mind. He could remember a bare cell where he and Willard had been imprisoned—that, and one other thing.

A picture of Doc Willard stretched on an altar, while Garth lifted a gleaming, razor sharp knife above his friend's breast.

He remembered that, but no more. It was enough.

The question burning in his brain had nearly wrecked his sanity. He had tried to get back into the Black Forest, to find Willard, dead or alive, to learn what had happened—to discover the answer to his problem. He had failed.

A year later he learned that his fiancée, Moira, had died of the Silver Plague. And he knew that Willard might have saved her, had he lived and continued his research.

After that, Ed Garth hit the skids. He went down fast, stopping only when he reached the bottom.

He killed the bottle and threw it out into emptiness, watching yellow light glint on glass as it dropped.

Well, he had his chance now. An expedition going into the Black Forest. But Garth was no longer the same husky giant who had fought his way through that deadly jungle.

Five years on the skids had played havoc with him. Stamina was gone. And the Black Forest was as terrible, as powerful, as ever.

Garth wished he had brought another bottle.

CHAPTER TWO

JUPITER is a ball of luminous clouded marble, gigantic in the sky of Ganymede. Its light is a queer, pale glow that lacks the warm brilliance of sunlight. When the titanic planet lifts over the horizon, gravity seems to shift, and the ground feels unstable beneath your feet.

Jupiter was rising now. Oretown lay ugly and desolate in the strange dawn. Across the plain where the spaceship had landed a string of truck-cats, big silvery desert freighters, stood motionless, ready to start the trip. There were signs of activity. At the central port of the *Hunter* stood a lanky, gray-haired man with a clipped, stiff Van Dyke. Behind him was Captain Brown.

Garth, his medical kit strapped to his back, ploughed through the light film of snow that lay over the sand. He was shivering in his thin garments, wishing he had a drink. Neither Brown nor his companion saw Garth's approach. The gray-haired man was speaking.

"—time to start. If this guide of yours doesn't show up, we'll have to wait till we find another."

"He'll show up," Brown said. "I only gave him ten bucks."

Garth reached the foot of the ramp leading up to the port-valve. " 'Morning. Am I late?"

There was no answer. He climbed the slope, slippery with snow despite the skid-treads, and stopped before the two men. Brown nodded at him.

"Here's our guide. Commander Benson." Benson scowled incredulously under tufted brows. "What the devil! You—you're an Earthman!"

"Sure," Garth said. "What about it?" The Commander glanced at Brown. "I expected a native. I didn't know—" He left the sentence hanging. "You can't wear those rags, man. Captain, break out some clothes for him." Without another look at Garth, Benson hurried down the ramp, shouting orders to someone below.

Brown grinned at the other. "Come on inside," he urged, and, in a lower tone, "He's the big shot. You know enough to keep your mouth shut—eh?"

Garth nodded. Brown peered at him sharply.

"You need coffee. I'll lace it. Come along." He took Garth to the galley, and, presently, supplied food, drink, and clothing. He lit a cigarette, idly watching the smoke sucked into the air-conditioning grill.

"Benson's a tough egg," he said at last "If he had the slightest idea we were figuring on—what we're figuring on, there'd be trouble. The Commander never takes chances. We've got to give him the slip, somehow."

Garth gulped coffee. "How many men do you have?"

"Ten."

"Not many."

"Fully armed, though. There are sixty in the expedition altogether, but I could only feel sure of ten. Some of them I planted myself."

Garth took the cigarette Brown handed him. "Thanks...I know Chahnn pretty well. Once we get there, we can get away from the others."

"How?"

"Underground passages—not well known. We'll come out about thirty miles from Chahnn, and from there it's another twenty to the Black Forest."

"The last lap on open ground?"

"Yeah."

"Not so good. If Benson misses us, he'll have planes out scouting. I've a hunch he's suspicious already."

"If he catches up with us, so what? There'll be other chances."

"That's what you think," Brown said grimly. "I told you Benson was a tough egg. He'd clap us all in the brig and we'd end up with prison sentences on Earth—hazarding the success of a planetary expedition, they call it. So you see why we've got to find this treasure, whatever it is."

"Then you don't know either, eh?"

"Maybe I've a few ideas... Finished? Let's go, then." Brown came to his feet.

GARTH followed Brown out of the ship, pondering. The Ancients had, admittedly, been an incredibly advanced race. Any treasure they thought worth guarding would be plenty valuable. Gold? Gems? They seemed trivial, compared to the tremendous scientific powers of the Ancients. And unimportant as well, while the Silver Plague raged over Earth.

They moved along the string of truck-cats, each loaded with the necessary equipment, and reached the first. Commander Benson was already there, talking to the pilot. He looked around.

"Ready? What's your name—Garth? All right, get in."

The front compartment of the truck-cat was roomy enough. Paula Trent, Garth saw, was already there. She gave no sign that she noticed him. He shrugged and found a seat, and Captain Brown dropped beside him, impassive as ever.

The pilot came in. "Sit up here, next to me, buddy," he ordered. "I'll need your help wrestling this tank through the arroyos."

Benson himself was the last man to enter. He slid the door shut and nodded. "Warm her up."

Beside the driver, Garth could not see the others, nor could he hear their conversation as the motors coughed and snarled into life. The truck-cat lurched forward on her caterpillar treads. The pilot looked inquiringly at Garth.

"Where'll I head? West? What about these quicksands I've been hearing about?"

"Steer for that mountain peak 'way over there," Garth told him. "It's easy to see the sink-holes. They're big grey patches on the sand, with no snow on 'em."

The roar of the engine died into a monotonous murmur. It was possible to hear the conversation in the rear of the compartment. Commander Benson was talking.

"—atomic power. It must have been that; there's no other answer. All we need to know is the nature of the booster charge."

"I don't get it," Paula said. "Booster charge?"

"As far as our physicists know, atomic power's possible if there's a known way to start it and control it. Earth's reserves are nearly exhausted. Oil, coal—used up almost completely. And Earth needs power plenty bad, to maintain civilization."

"The other planets have fuel."

"Space shipping's too expensive. It's prohibitive, Paula. Unless a new power source is found very soon, Earthmen may have to migrate to another world—and our civilization's so complex that that's nearly impossible. Maybe we can find the answer in Chahnn this time. It was one of the biggest cities of the Ancients."

"I've never seen it," Captain Brown said.

BENSON grunted. "I did, once. Years ago. Tremendous! The scientific achievements they must have had! And nobody knows what happened to the Ancients. They just vanished, and their machines kept running till they'd used up their power—and stopped. So there's no trace left. We've located the fuel chambers, but in every case they've been empty. Experiments have been made—unsuccessfully."

"You still think my translation of the Harro Panel was wrong, eh?" Paula put in.

"I do," Commander Benson said. "It was a variable cipher. No one else agrees with you that it was a code map."

"Ever heard of a double code?"

"I'm sorry," Benson said shortly. "We've settled all this. The Black Forest is impassable. We can't risk our chance of success on a wild goose chase."

Beside the pilot, Garth's mouth twisted sardonically. He had an idea now of what Carver Brown and Paula were after. The secret of the Ancients' power-source. Well, it might be found in the Black Forest. Anything might. Including the lost race of the Zarno, and... His eyes went hard. Not yet would he let himself believe Doc Willard was still alive. The most he could hope for was an answer to that question—the tormenting problem of whether or not he had killed Willard.

Lost in his absorption, he snapped out of it scarcely in time as the truck-cat skidded on slick ice.

"Hard left! Sand the treads!" Instinctively his hand flashed to the right lever, releasing a sprinkling of sand that provided traction. He held it down while the pilot fought the wheel. They lurched, swung half around, and found level surface again. Through the window Garth could see a twenty-foot-wide funnel, sloping down to a black hole at the center.

"What was it?" the pilot asked.

"*Creethas,* the natives call 'em, but that doesn't mean much. Six-foot insects. Poisonous. They dig traps like ant-lions on Earth, pits with sloping sides. Once you skid on the ice, you slip on down to the hole at the bottom."

"Dangerous?"

"Not to us, in here. But we might have damaged the engine."

"Keep your eyes open after this, Garth," Commander Benson said sharply.

"Okay." Garth was silent. The truck-cat drove on, leading the procession.

The vehicles were fast. On level ground they raced, hitting eighty m.p.h. sometimes. By Jupiter-set they had reached Chahnn. Paula, for one, was disappointed.

"I expected a city," she told Garth as they stared around at the mile-square block of black stone, raised a few feet above ground level, its surface broken by a few structures oddly reminiscent of the subway kiosks of two centuries ago.

"It's all underground," Garth said. He was feeling shaky, needing a shot or two of liquor. But there was none. In lieu of it, he borrowed a cigarette from the girl and idled about, watching the men make camp.

THE ROOMY truck-cats provided accommodations for sixty men without crowding. It wasn't necessary to set up tents. Indeed, in that icy air, only "warmer" tents, heated by induced current in their metallic fabric, would have been feasible. The trucks, however, could be heated easily and were air-conditioned. Garth walked over to a kiosk and peered into the black depths. Chahnn lay below, the gigantic, complicated city of the Ancients.

Through Chahnn was the road to the Black Forest—the only road they could use, under the circumstances.

Garth shivered and went in search of Brown. He was feeling shakier than ever. Vividly in his mind was a picture he did not want to remember—a man stretched on an altar, a knife at his breast...

He found Brown beside one of the trucks, looking into the darkness.

"Captain—"

"Huh? Oh, Garth. Say, Paula—Miss Trent took a flashlamp and went down into Chahnn to do a bit of exploring. I was thinking of going after her. Any danger down there?"

Garth shook his head. "It's a dead city. She'll be okay."

"Unless she gets lost."

"She won't. There are markers pointing to the outlets. How about a drink? I could use one."

Scowling, Brown nodded and pushed Garth into the truck. "I bunk in here, with the Commander. You'll have to find a place with the men, somewhere. Oh, by the way—" He pushed folded slips into Garth's hand. "Here's the rest of that forty. And here's a drink."

Garth gulped brandy better than any he had tasted in years. He didn't bother with a glass. Brown watched him with an almost imperceptible curl of the lip.

"Thanks... When do I get that ten thousand?"

"When we're back here. I don't trust you quite enough to let you have it now."

Garth wiped his mouth with the back of his hand, considered, and drank again. "I won't run out on you. You're after that Ancients' power-source, aren't you?"

Brown's eyes narrowed a bit. "Any of your business?"

"Not in the way you mean. But I know the Black Forest. I might be able to give you some ideas, if I'm not left too much in the dark. Still, I can guess a little. I know you expect to run into the Zarno."

"Yeah?"

Garth made an impatient gesture. "Hell, why did you want me as a guide? It wasn't only because I knew the Forest. I can speak the Ancient Tongue—the same language the Zarno are supposed to use. You'll want me to palaver with them."

"Maybe." Brown went to the back of the truck and found a fresh pack of cigarettes. "We can talk about that later."

"We ought to talk now. I know what sort of equipment you'll need in the Forest. If you run out on Benson half-equipped, it'll be just too bad."

The door swung open, admitting a blast of frigid air. Commander Benson stepped in, his lips tight and hard, his eyes blazing. Brown, at the end of the chamber, swung around, a sudden, surprised tenseness in his attitude.

"I don't think you'll do any running out on me, Captain," Benson said.

Brown flashed Garth a glance. "Damn you," he half-whispered. He took a step forward, tigerishly menacing.

BENSON pulled a gun from his pocket.

"Don't move," he said. "Hold it right there. I thought you'd given up that crazy idea you and Paula had, but apparently—" He shrugged. "Well, I'll have to put you and the girl under guard. No one in this outfit's heading for the Black Forest if I can help it."

Brown's hand hovered in midair.

"Don't try it," Benson said. "Keep your gun where it belongs. The sound of a shot wouldn't help you any." He stepped back, his mouth opening in a shout that would summon others.

Brown, at the other end of the truck, could not have reached him in time, but the Commander had forgotten or ignored Garth. That was a mistake. Garth was only a few feet from Benson, and he galvanized into unexpected action. He sprang, one hand clamping over the gun, the other, clenched, driving in a hard, short jab at Benson's chin.

There was strength in that punch, and it connected at the right point. Had Garth not been gripping the Commander's hand, the latter would have gone backward, out of the truck.

"Knockout!" Brown said tonelessly. He was suddenly beside Garth, yanking Benson forward. "Shut the door. Quick."

Garth obeyed. Turning, he saw the Captain kneeling beside Benson's motionless form. After a moment Brown looked up.

"He'll come out of it soon. Maybe too soon. Get me those straps from the corner."

Garth did that, and then had another drink. He felt lousy. He watched Brown bind the Commander and thrust the lax figure out of sight, under a bunk.

"That does it," Brown said, rising. "We're in the soup now. But—it was lucky you hit him when you did."

"What now?"

"We start for the Black Forest before Benson wakes up. I'm second in command. I'll get my own men, and we'll jump the gun." Brown's eyes were excited.

"Equipment?"

"We'll take what we can. Weapons, mostly. Stay with me."

They went out of the truck into the soft light of four moons, two large, two tiny. Fourfold shadows paced them over the icy slick. Garth hurried off to find his medical kit. By the time he returned, Brown had mustered his men and was waiting. He gave Garth a brief glance.

"Okay. Morgan—" He turned to a giant in uniform. "I'll be back in a couple of hours. As soon as we find Miss Trent. 'Bye."

" 'Bye, sir."

Garth led the way into one of the kiosks. Lamps were flashed on. A spiral ramp led steeply down.

In an undertone Brown said, "I told Morgan Commander Benson sent me to find Paula Trent—that she was lost in the city. So we're safe till—"

"We're safe till we leave the underground passage," Garth said. "After that, twenty miles across open ground. Has Benson got planes?"

"Portable ones, yeah."

"Then we'd better do that twenty miles at night."

The ramp ended. Before them was a gigantic room where their tiny lamps were lost. Here and there enigmatic shadows loomed, the dead, fantastic machines of the Ancients that had once made Chahnn alive and powerful.

GARTH went directly to an opening in the wall—Brown and his ten men following—and entered a short tunnel. At one spot he paused, ran his finger over a panel of smooth metal, and pressed. A black oval opened silently.

"Here's the way. They won't follow us beyond this point."

Brown nodded. "Sampson, get the men inside. Wait here for me. I'll be back as soon as I can."

A burly, beak-nosed fellow with a cast in one eye and flaming red hair saluted casually. "Right. Come on, boys. Hop through. Mind your packs."

Garth stared at Brown. "What d'you mean? Where—"

The Captain said, "We're taking Paula Trent with us."

"No! It's nearly suicide for us—she couldn't make it at all."

"She's tougher than you think. Besides, she's got the map. And she's an archaeologist. I can't read the Ancients' lingo. Can you?"

Garth shook his head. "I can speak it, that's all. But—"

"If we find what we're after, we'll need Paula Trent. She's down here somewhere. Let's go find her."

"I tell you—"

Brown brought out a gun and leveled it.

"Find her. Or I'll find her myself, and we'll head for the Black Forest without you. Because you'll be dead. I haven't come this far to let you stop me. And chivalry looks a bit funny on a guy like you."

Sudden murder-light flared in the pale eyes.

"Find her!" Brown whispered. "And fast!"

CHAPTER THREE

GARTH knuckled under. There was nothing else to do. He knew Brown wouldn't hesitate to kill him, and, after all, what the devil did Paula Trent mean to him? Her life was unimportant, compared to the hopeless quest that had quickened in his mind, despite himself.

For Doc Willard might still be alive. Even if he wasn't, there was that notebook the Doc had always carried around with him—a hook that contained the medico's theories about the Silver Plague. Even if that ghastly dream-like memory were not merely delirium—even if Garth, witless and unknowing, had killed Willard—there was always that dim, desperate chance that the cure for the Plague might be found in the Black Forest.

So—damn Paula Trent! She didn't matter, when the lives of millions might depend on Garth's penetrating the jungle that had baffled him for five years.

Without a word he turned and started back, Brown keeping close beside him. The huge chamber loomed before them, filled with its cryptic shadows. There was time now to see what they had missed in their quick flight a few moments ago—though not much time, for pursuit might start at any minute. Dead silence, and darkness, broken by the crossing beams of the brilliant lamps. Garth listened.

"Hear anything?"

Brown shook his head.

"Nothing."

"Okay. We'll try this way."

Then went into a passage that sloped down, ending in a vaulted room larger than the first. Brown swung up his gun abruptly as a figure seemed to leap from blackness in the ray of the lamp. Garth caught his arm.

"Robot. Unpowered. They're all over the city."

The robots—slaves of the Ancients, Garth thought, who had died with them, lacking the fuel that could quicken them to life. No Earthly scientists had ever been able to analyze the construction of the machines, for they were built of an alloy that was apparently indestructible. Acid and flame made no impression on the smooth, glittering black surface.

This one, like all the others, was roughly man-shaped, nearly eight feet tall, and with four arms, the hands extended into limber jointed fingers almost like tendencies. From the mask-like face complex glassy eyes stared blankly. It stood motionless, guarding a world that no longer needed guardians.

With a little shrug Garth went on, his ears alert for sounds. From the walls bizarre figures in muraled panels watched. Those murals showed a world of incredibly advanced science, Garth knew. He had seen them before. He spared them not a glance now.

The machines—

What were they? They loomed like dinosaurs in the endless chain of high-domed vaults. They had once given Chahnn power and life and strength. The murals showed that. The Ancient Race had used antigravity—a secret unknown to Earthmen—and they had created food by the rearrangement of atomic patterns, not even requiring hydroponic tank cultures. They had ruled this world like gods.

And they had passed with no trace, leaving only these silent monuments to their greatness. With the power of the Ancients, Earth's lack of fuel-reserves would not matter. If the secret of atomic power could be found again, these machines would roar into thundering life—and machines like them would rise on Earth.

Power and greatness such as civilization had never known! Power even to reach the stars!

And—Garth thought wryly—a power that would be useless unless a cure for the Silver Plague could be found.

HE WAS almost running now, his footsteps and Brown's echoing hollowly in the great rooms. Silently he cursed Paula Trent. There were other levels below, many of them, and she might be down there—which would make the task almost impossible.

A distant flicker of light jerked Garth to a halt. He switched off his lamp, motioning for Brown to do the same.

It came again, far away, a firefly glimpse. "Paula?" the Captain said.

"Guess so. Unless they're after us already."

"Take it easy, then."

They went on, running lightly on their toes. The light had vanished, but Garth knew the way. Suddenly they came out of a short tunnel into one of the great rooms, and relief flooded Garth as he saw Paula's face, pale in reflected light, a dozen feet away.

Simultaneously a faint sound came rhythmically—like dim drums.

Garth said sharply, "Hear that? Men coming down a ramp. Get the girl and let's go!"

But Paula was already coming toward them, blinking in the glare. "Who's that? Carver? I—"

Brown gripped her arm. "There's no time to talk now, Paula. We're in a jam. Keep your mouth shut and come along. Garth, can you get us back to that secret passage?"

"Maybe. It'll be blind luck if we make it. Turn your lamps out and link hands. Here." He felt Paula's firm, warm palm hard against his, and remembrance of Moira was suddenly unexpectedly painful. He had not seen an Earth girl for years...

What of it, now? Garth moved cat-footedly forward, leading the others. He went fast. Once or twice he clicked on his light briefly. They could hear the noise of the search party now, and a few times, could see distant lights.

"If they find that open panel—" Brown whispered.

"Keep quiet."

Garth pressed them back into an alcove as footsteps grew louder. Luck stayed with them. The searchers turned off at another passage. After that...

It was like a nightmare, a blind, stumbling race through the blackness of Chahnn, with menace hiding everywhere. Garth's hand was slippery with perspiration against Paula's by the time he stopped, his light clicking on and off again almost instantly.

"This is it," he said. "The panel's shut."

"Good. Sampson must have had sense enough to close it. Unless—"

Garth found the spring and pressed it. He flashed his light into the darkness, to see the familiar faces of Brown's men staring at him. The Captain thrust him forward. Paula was instantly beside him, and then Brown himself was through the oval gap.

"They're coming," he murmured. "How in hell does this work?"

"Here." Garth didn't use his light. Under his deft fingers the panel slid back into place, shutting off the noise of approaching steps. He gasped a little with relief.

"Okay," he said in a natural voice. "These walls are sound-proof. We can use our lights. We'll have to."

"What happened?" Paula's voice said. "You said we were in a jam, Carver. Well?"

"We'll talk as we go. Garth, you first. Paula, stay with me. Sampson, bring up the rear, will you?"

GARTH obediently set out down the sloping tunnel, scarcely listening to Brown's explanation. There were side branches to the passage here and there. He had to use his memory, which seemed less accurate than he remembered. Once he almost blundered, but caught himself in time.

Brown said, "Garth, we've got thirty miles of tunnel and twenty more above ground till we hit the Forest. Right? This is rough going. We won't get out of here till daylight. So we'd better camp in the passage, at the other end, till tomorrow night."

"We don't have to do that," Garth grunted. "This isn't Earth. Jupiter won't rise for thirteen hours."

"The men have heavy packs." Brown shifted his own big one uncomfortably. "Fifty miles is quite a way. Still, the quicker we reach the Forest, the safer we'll be."

"There's a river." Garth's voice was doubtful. "We might use that."

"Would it help?"

"Yeah. But it's dangerous."

"Why?"

"Spouts. Geysers. The water's apt to explode under you any time. And there are big lizards—"

"Would it take long to make a raft?"

Garth shook his head. "*Lata*-trees are better than balsa, and they grow on the banks. Plenty of vines, too. But—"

"We'll do that, then," Brown said decisively. "Speed it up. We've got thirteen hours. We can make it, all right."

Garth didn't answer.

After that it was pure monotony, a dull driving march through a bare tunnel, up slopes and down them, till leg muscles were aching with fatigue. Garth dropped into a state of tired apathy. He had no pack to carry, but nevertheless his liquor-soaked body rebelled at the unaccustomed exertion. But he knew that each step brought him closer to his goal.

The thoughts swung monotonously through his brain. Doc Willard. The notebook. The cure. The Plague. Maybe—maybe—*maybe!*

If he got through—if he found the notebook—if it had the cure—that was what he wanted, of course.

But suppose he also found the skeleton of Doc Willard on an altar, with a knife hilt protruding from the ribs?

He couldn't have killed Doc consciously. That was unthinkable. Yet the damnable influence of the Noctoli pollen did odd things to a man's mind.

Doc Willard...Moira...the Silver Plague...

Half asleep, aching with exhaustion, he slogged ahead, moving like an automaton. And, whenever he slowed his pace, Brown's sharp voice urged him on faster.

Grudgingly the Captain allowed them rest periods. But by the time they reached the tunnel's end the men were panting and sweating, and both Paula and Garth were near exhaustion. Thirty miles at a fast pace, with only occasional rests, is wearing work.

THEY emerged from the passage to find themselves on the slope of a rocky hillock. Low ridges rose around them, silhouetted in triple-moonlight. A whitish haze hung close to the ground, filling the hollows like shining water.

Instinctively Brown looked up. A meteor, drawn by the immense gravity of Jupiter, flamed across the sky—that was all. And that was a familiar enough sight.

Garth, reeling with fatigue, nodded. "River—down there. Half a mile. The fog's thicker—"

"Okay. Let's go."

This lap of the journey was nearly the hardest. But the low roar of the river steadily grew louder as they stumbled on, the luminous mist lapping their ankles, their knees, their waists. It closed above their heads, so that they moved in a ghostlike, shadowless world in which the very air seemed dimly lighted.

Trees were visible. Garth, almost spent, searched for a shelving beach, found it, and dropped in a limp heap. He saw Paula sink down beside him. The men threw off their heavy packs with relief.

Brown—the man was made of rawhide and steel!—said, "I'll need help to make a raft. The boys that feel tired can keep their eyes open for pursuit planes. I don't think the Commander would send out truck-cats at night, but he'll use searching planes."

"They can't see us in this fog," Paula said faintly.

"They could hear us, with their motors muffled. So we'll work fast. Garth!"

"Yeah. What?"

"What trees do we want?"

Garth pointed. "*Lata.* Like that one, over there. They're easy to cut down, and they float. You'll find tough vines all around here." He forced the words out with an effort. Brown mustered eight of his men, including the red-haired Sampson, and led them away. The sound of ringing axes presently drifted back.

Two others had been stationed on hillocks, above the low-lying fog, to watch for planes. Garth, alone with Paula, was almost too tired to be conscious of her presence. He heard her voice.

"Cigarette?"

"Thanks..." Garth took one.

"Sorry I can't offer you a drink."

"So am I," Garth grunted. He could feel her eyes on him. He drew the smoke deep into his lungs, exhaling luxuriously.

"Got a gun?"

"Yes. Why?"

"Oh—things come out of the river sometimes. Hunting water-lizards, carnivorous. You learn to sleep with one eye open on Ganymede."

"It's a funny world," Paula acknowledged. "Once it was highly civilized. Now it's gone back to savagery."

"Conditions are bad here. Too vigorous. Jupiter gives light but not much heat. Animals and plants have to be tough to survive. This is summer-season, but it's plenty cold."

"How much do you know about the Zarno?" she asked abruptly.

Garth blinked. "Not much. Why?"

"Not many people have ever seen them. I'm wondering. I managed to translate some inscriptions from Chahnn... The Zarno aren't human, are they?"

Garth didn't answer. Paula went on.

"The Ancients knew them, though. They tried to educate them—like Rome colonizing savage races. That's probably why the Zarno are supposed to speak the Ancient Tongue."

"They do."

"And then the Ancients died out—somehow. The Zarno were left. They became barbarous again. I wish I knew what they were like. Natives who've seen them don't seem able to describe the creatures. They wear shining armor, don't they?"

GARTH closed his eyes, trying to remember. A vague, dim picture was growing in his mind—man-like figures that glowed, faces that were craggy, hideous creatures...

"I've seen them," he said, "but I've forgotten. The Noctoli poison—it wrecked my memory."

"You don't recall anything?"

"I—" Garth rubbed his forehead. "Not human—no. Creatures like living statues, shining and moving...I don't know."

"Silicate life?" Paula theorized thoughtfully. "It's possible. And it might evolve on a planet where conditions are so tough for survival. Such creatures wouldn't be affected by the Noctoli pollen, either, would they?"

"No. Or they've built up resistance. The virus is active only in daylight, when the flowers are open. I don't know why. Before we go too far into the Black Forest I'll have to give everyone antitoxin shots—everyone but me. The pollen doesn't work on me anymore."

They were silent, resting. It seemed only a moment before Brown appeared, announcing that the raft was ready.

"It's a makeshift job, but it's strong," he said. "Listen, Garth, what about the planes spotting us on the river? We'll be an easy target."

"They wouldn't fire on us?"

"No. But they'd use sleep-gas, and nab us when we drifted ashore. We don't want that."

Garth rose, his muscles aching. "It's a chance. Most of the time there'll be fog on the river. That'll help." He found his medical kit and shouldered it. "I'm ready."

The men were already on the raft, a big platform of light, tough *lata*-logs bound together by vines. Garth took his place near the pile of equipment in the center. "Keep to midstream," he cautioned. "Watch for bubbles breaking ahead. Swing wide of those. Waterspouts."

The raft slid out from the bank, long poles guiding it. Water washed aboard and slipped away as the platform found its balance. Presently they were drifting downstream in the dimly lighted fog, the black river murmuring quietly beneath them.

Garth kept his gaze ahead. It was hard to see in the faint, filtered light of the moons, but a ray-lamp would have been betraying to any planes that might be searching above.

"Swing left. Hard," he called.

The men obeyed. Oily bubbles were breaking the surface. As the raft moved toward the bank, a sudden geyser burst up from the river, a spouting torrent that tipped the platform dangerously and showered its occupants with icy spray.

Garth met Brown's eyes. "See what I mean?" he remarked.

"Yeah. Still, if that's all—"

The river flowed fast. Once or twice the plated back of a giant saurian was visible, but the water-reptiles did not attack, made wary, perhaps, by the bulk of the raft. There were other waterspouts, but the men soon became adept at avoiding them.

Sometimes they drifted through fog; sometimes the mists were dissipated by winds, though not often. During one of the latter periods a faint droning drifted down from above. It was the worst possible timing, for the two larger moons were directly overhead, blazing down on the river. The stub-winged shape of a plane loomed against the starry sky.

Brown said sharply, "Drop flat. Don't move." He forced Garth and Paula down. "No, don't look up. They'd see our faces."

"They can't miss us," Sampson muttered.

"There's fog ahead."

The sound of the plane's motors grew louder. Abruptly there was a splash. Another. Something shattered on the raft.

"Hold your breath!" Brown snapped.

Garth tried to obey. A stinging ache had crept into his nostrils. His lungs began to hurt. The plane had spotted them—that was obvious. Sleep-gas works fast.

CRYPT-CITY of the DEATHLESS ONE

A grimly-stirring novel of weird adventure on an alien world

by

HENRY KUTTNER

Another soft crash. Garth scarcely heard it. He saw a stubby, cruciform shadow sweep over the raft, as the plane swooped, and then the wall of silvery fog was looming up ahead. Paula gave a little gasp. Her body collapsed against him.

The fire in Garth's chest was blazing agony. Despite himself, he let breath rush into his lungs.

After that, complete blackness and oblivion.

CHAPTER FOUR

GARTH woke in reddish, dim twilight. Instantly he knew where he was, even before he sat up and saw the black boles of immense trees rising like pillars around him. The Forest!

"About time," Captain Brown's toneless voice said. "That sleep-gas put you under for hours."

Garth rose, glancing around. They were camped in a little clearing among the gigantic trees, and some of the men were heating their rations over radiolite stove kits. From above, the crimson light filtered vaguely from a leafy roof incredibly far. The trees of the Black Forest were taller than California sequoias, and Jupiter light reached the ground faintly, through the ceiling of red leaves that roofed the jungle. Paula, Garth saw, was lying with her eyes closed not far away.

"She all right?"

"Sure," Brown said. "Resting is all. We got away from Benson's plane—hit that fog bank just in time. You'd passed out, so I took a chance and kept going. After we reached the Forest, I landed the raft and headed inland a bit. So here we are."

Garth nodded. "That was wise. The river goes underground a half mile further. Any—accidents?"

Brown looked at him oddly. "This might be Yosemite, for all the danger I've seen so far. It's a picnic."

"That," Garth said, "is just why it's so bad. You don't see the trouble till after it's happened." He didn't explain. "Where's my kit?"

"Here. Why?"

"Before we go any further, we'll need shots. Antitoxin against the Noctoli pollen. The flowers don't grow on the edges of the Forest, but the wind carries their poison quite a ways sometimes." Garth rummaged in his kit, found sealed vials and a hypo, and carefully sterilized everything over a radiolite stove he commandeered from one of the men. After that, he administered the antivirus, first to Paula and last of all to Brown. He took none himself; he had acquired a natural immunity to the pollen.

There was barely enough to go around. Brown's shot was slightly less than the regular dosage, which vaguely worried Garth. But the Captain, annoyed by the delay, was anxious to talk about immediate plans.

"Benson might land at the edge of the Forest and come after us a mile or so. Not further. But we'd better start moving." He led Garth over to where Paula sat. "It's time for you to see the map."

The girl nodded in agreement. She took out a folded flex-paper and extended it. Garth squinted down in the red twilight.

"Map?"

"More like a treasure hunt," Paula explained. "There's a series of guide-points, you see. So far we're okay—*narva* means west, in the Ancient Tongue, doesn't it?"

"*Narva.*" Garth gave the word a slightly different pronunciation. "Yeah. Well—three *sallags* north-west to the Mouths of the Waters Below—"

"Mouths of the Singing Below, I made it."

Garth shook his head. "I can't read the stuff. I just know the spoken language. Read the whole thing out loud, so I can get it."

Paula obeyed. Her pronunciation made some words unfamiliar to Garth, but by experiment he found what was meant.

"Uh-huh. A *sallag* is less than three miles, as far as I can judge. I think I know the place. It's a hill honeycombed with little caves. You can hear water running underneath it."

"That fits," the girl agreed. "This won't be so hard, after all."

Garth grunted. He turned to Brown.

"I want a gun. And a knife. I'll need both."

"Sampson!"

The red-haired man approached, squinting. "Yeah?"

"Rustle up a knife and gun for Garth."

"Check."

Paula was staring at Garth. "You expect trouble, don't you?"

"I do."

She made a gesture. "This all seems so peaceful—"

"LISTEN," Garth said, "the Black Forest is the worst death-trap in the System. Here's why. The struggle for existence is plenty tough here. Brute strength isn't enough, nor agility. A tiger or a deer wouldn't last long here. In the Forest, the survival of the fittest means the plant or animal that can get the most food. That sort of thing has been going on here for a million years. The beasts developed super-quick reactions. They could smell danger a mile away. So they had to have strength, agility, and something else—to get close to their prey."

Brown stared. "What?"

"Invisibility. Or its equivalent. Ever heard of protective coloration? Camouflage? Well, the creatures of the Forest are the most perfect camouflage experts that exist. They don't simply trick your eyes, either. They trick the other senses. If you smell perfume, take it easy, or you'll find yourself asleep, while your head's being chewed off by a lizard that looks as nasty as it smells good. If you see a path and it feels solid, don't walk too far on it. Things have made that path. A carnivorous moss that feels exactly like smooth dirt underfoot—till their digestive juices start working. If you hear me yelling your name, take it easy. There are birds like harpies here that imitate sounds the way parrots do."

Garth's grin was tight. "You'll find out. It's camouflage carried to the last degree, for offense and defense. I know the Forest pretty well; you don't. You haven't developed a sort of sixth sense—an instinct—that tells you when something smells bad, even though it looks like a six-course dinner."

"All right," the Captain said. "This is your territory, not mine. It's up to you."

It was. Garth decided later as he led the way through the black columns of the trees, very much up to him. Brown and the others were tough, hard fighters, but they didn't know the subtleties of this hellhole, where death lurked everywhere disguised. He had got a drink from Sampson and his nerves were less jagged, but physical exhaustion still gripped him. He'd been on the skids for a long time, and was in rotten bad shape. But if the girl could stand it, he could.

It was warmer in the Forest; the trees seemed to exhale heat and moisture, and there was no snow on the ground. Great ebony pillars of giant trees, rising hundreds of feet into the air, made the place a labyrinth. And the deceptive reddish twilight made walking difficult, even to Garth's trained senses.

There was trouble, though. When a gorgeously colored butterfly, flame-red and green, fluttered down toward Paula, Garth hastily slapped at the insect with a thick leaf he was carrying. "Watch out for those," he told the girl, nodding toward the crushed body. "They're poisonous. Bad medicine."

And once, as Brown was about to seat himself on a rounded grayish boulder, Garth whirled the man away just in time. A hole in the rock gaped open, and a pair of fanged mandibles snapped out, clicking together viciously. Garth put a bullet in the thing. It heaved itself up on spidery legs, revealing that the "rock" was a carapace covering an insect-like body. And it took a long time to die.

There were other, similar incidents. They had a bad effect on the men, even Sampson. The crew Brown had picked was tough, but the Black Forest was like distilled poison. It was easier to face a charging rhino than to travel through this ebony jungle where silent, secret death lurked concealed, in a diabolic masquerade.

That was the first day. The second was worse. The trees were thicker, and sometimes it was necessary to use *machete* blades to hew through the tangled undergrowth.

ANOTHER DAY—and another—and another, following the clues on Paula's cipher map. They found the first guidepost—the hill honeycombed with caves—and from there went on to the east, camping at the edge of a ravine that dropped away into unplumbed darkness.

Camouflage-moss grew here, looking deceptively like solid ground. One of the men ventured too close to the edge of the cleft, and the moss crumbled beneath him, dropping him into a nest of the roots—twining, writhing cannibalistic serpents with sucker-disks that drank bloodthirstily.

They got him out in time, luckily. But the men's nerves were jolted.

After that, day after day, constant alertness was vital. The party walked with guns and knives in their hands. Their footsteps rang hollow in the dead, empty silence of the Forest...

It was only Garth's knowledge of the dark wilderness that got them through to the interior. After a week, he was further in than he had ever penetrated before, except when he had crashed the air-car with Doc Willard five years ago.

But they were getting closer—nearer! More and more often Garth remembered the black notebook that might hold the cure for the Silver Plague. For some indefinable reason he had come to feel that Paula's goal was also his.

It was logical enough. They were searching for a lost treasure house of the Ancient Race, guarded, perhaps, by the Zarno. And Garth was certain that, during that period of partial amnesia, he and Willard had been captives of the Zarno. He had been drugged with the Noctoli poison by day, but at night he had wakened in a bare cell with his friend—a cell with walls of metal, he recalled. It had been windowless. Lighted by a faint glow from one comer.

It checked. A ruin, once built by the Ancients, now inhabited by the Zarno.

If he could find that notebook...

He always stopped there. He knew what he might also discover—the skeleton of Willard, stretched on an altar. That picture always made his stomach go cold and tight.

That night Brown complained of a splitting headache. They camped near a stream, and Garth accompanied the Captain down to the bank, with canvas pails. Jupiter was invisible—they had not seen the sky for a week—but the red light was fading.

"Not too close," Garth cautioned. "Let me test it first."

Brown stared at him. "What now? I'm getting to expect anything here." The man's expressionless face showed signs of strain and exhaustion. He had no nerves, apparently, but the grueling journey had told on him nevertheless.

Garth used his knife to cut down a sapling. He impaled a leaf on its point and extended it gingerly over the dark water. After a moment he felt a shock like a striking fish, and the pole was nearly wrenched from his hands. And he wrestled with it; Brown's hands gripped the sapling.

"What the devil! Garth—"

"Let it go. I was only testing, anyway." The pole was dragged into the water, where it thrashed about violently for a few moments.

"What is it?"

GARTH was searching through the underbrush for something. "Water snakes. Big ones—perfectly transparent. They wait for some animal to come along and take a drink. Then—bang!" He nodded. "Here we are. We'll find a lot of the Noctoli flowers from now on."

He brought out a bloom nearly a foot in diameter, with leaves of pulpy, glossy black, a thick powdering of silver in its cup. "This is Noctoli, Captain. Looks harmless, doesn't it?"

"Yeah." Brown rubbed his forehead. "The pollen gives you amnesia?"

"In the daytime, when it's active. It's phototropic—needs light. Jupiter can't have set yet, so this ought to work." Garth found another pole, speared the flower on its tip, and extended the blossom over the water. He shook the silver dust into the stream.

"It works fast. The snakes will be paralyzed in a few seconds. The current carries off the pollen, we dip up the water we need—and that's that."

Paula appeared through the bushes, glancing around warily. In the last week everyone had learned to be alert always. Lines of fatigue showed on her pale face. Red-gold hair was plastered damply on her forehead.

"Carver—"

"What's up?"

She glanced at Garth. "The men. Sampson's talking to them."

Brown's rat-trap mouth clamped tight. "That so? Sampson shoots off his mouth too much. What's the angle?"

"I think they want to go back."

Garth, dipping up water in the canvas buckets, said, "We've only three more days to go, unless we run into bad country."

"I know. But—they're armed."

"I'll talk to 'em," Brown said quietly. He lifted two of the pails and started up the path, Paula and Brown trailing him. Presently they reached the clearing where camp had been made.

The men weren't cooking. Instead, they were gathered in a knot around Sampson, whose blazing red hair stood up like a beacon. Brown put down his burden and walked toward them.

They broke up at sight of him, but didn't scatter. Sampson's hand crept imperceptibly toward his holster.

"Trouble?" Brown asked.

Sampson squinted at him. "No trouble. Except we didn't know the Forest would be as bad as it is."

"So you want to go back?"

"You can't blame us for that," Sampson said, hunching his heavy shoulders. "It's only dumb luck that's kept us alive so far. We didn't bargain for this, Captain."

"I told you what to expect."

"All you said was that it'd be dangerous. None of us knew the Forest. Those damn bloodsucker plants are the worst. They reach out at a guy everywhere he turns. And the other things—we can't get through, Captain! You ought to be able to see that yourself!"

"Nobody's been killed so far."

"Blind luck. And Garth, too. He knows this country. If we didn't have him, we wouldn't have lasted a day."

"We've got him," Brown said crisply. "So we're going on. Only three more days, anyhow. That's enough. Start cooking your rations." He turned his back on Sampson and walked away. The red-haired giant hesitated, scowling. Finally he shrugged and glanced around at the others.

That broke the tension. One by one the men scattered to prepare food.

Only Garth was gnawed by a persistent, deep-rooted fear. He didn't admit it, even to himself. But he watched Brown closely that night and finally unpacked his medical kit and carefully searched it for something he knew wasn't there.

He was dreading the next morning.

CHAPTER FIVE

SLOW reddish dawn brightened over the Forest. Garth felt someone shaking him. He grunted, stirred, and opened his eyes to see Paula's white face, and, behind her, Sampson.

"Yeah. What's wrong?" He scrambled out of his blankets, blinking. The girl, pale to the lips, pointed toward a recumbent figure.

"Carver. Captain Brown. He's—I don't know!"

Sampson said gruffly, "Looks like he's dead. The men on guard duty said he didn't move once all night."

Icy bands constricted suddenly around Garth's heart. Without answering he got his kit and went over to examine Brown. The man lay motionless, his breathing normal, but a deep flush on his brown cheeks.

"It isn't the Plague, is it?" Sampson asked, his voice not quite under control.

Garth shook his head. "Hell, no! It's—" He hesitated.

Paula caught his arm. "What? Some insect poisoned him—one of those butterfly-things?"

Garth carefully repacked his kit. He didn't look up.

"He's got a dose of the Noctoli pollen. That's all. It's not fatal. He'll come out of it after he leaves the Forest, or after he builds up immunity."

"How long would that take?"

"A month or more."

Garth bent over the apparently sleeping man. "Get up, Brown," he said insistently. "Hear me? Get up?"

The Captain stirred. His eyes opened, blank and unseeing. He drew himself from his blankets and rose, looking straight ahead. Paula shrank back with a little gasp. There was a flurry of movement among the men in the background.

"He'll be all right tonight. The poison only works in the daytime—I've told you that."

"We can't march at night," Paula said. "Not—here!"

"I know. It's impossible. Our lights would attract the butterflies—and plenty of other things."

Sampson whirled on the others. "Pack your equipment! We're getting out of here, fast!"

They hurried to obey. Paula got in front of Sampson as he turned, and the giant stopped, blinking at her.

"You can't leave the Captain here, Sampson."

"We'll carry him, then. But we're getting out."

Garth moved to Paula's side. "You won't need a litter. He can walk. Noctoli poison works like hypnotism. You're semi-conscious, but your will's in abeyance. If anyone tells Brown to follow us, he'll do it."

Paula was biting her lip. "We can't go back now. We've only three days to go."

"Look," Sampson said grimly, "why in hell should we commit suicide? Suppose we head on for three days. We reach this lost city of yours, or whatever it is. What then? We're in the middle of the Black Forest. Another thirteen days to get out! It's too much of a gamble. We're leaving now, and you can come along or stay here—suit yourself!" He turned away.

LEFT ALONE, Paula looked helplessly from the motionless, staring figure of Brown to Garth.

"Carver!"

He didn't move. Garth grinned wryly. "He'll obey commands, that's all. He won't wake up till tonight."

Paula clenched her hands. "We've got to go on! We've got to! If we go back now—"

"Commander Benson will clap us in the brig, eh?"

She looked at him angrily. "It isn't only that. We'd lose our chance. You were right. Garth—we're after the power-source of the Ancients. The secret's hidden here, in the Black Forest. That cipher from Chahnn proved that—to me, anyway. Earth needs power, more than you can imagine. Without it, civilization will collapse—soon, too."

"Suppose we go on," Garth said slowly. "I didn't tell you this, but the reason the poison hit Brown was because my antitoxin was too old. He had a short dose, too. The other men—well, they'll go under themselves in a day or so. You, too."

Blue smudges showed under the girl's eyes. "Oh," she said after a moment. "So it's like that."

"Just like that."

Paula's stubborn chin tilted up. "I don't care—there's still a way. We'll be all right at night, you said. Well, we'll do our traveling and fighting by night."

"Fighting?"

"The Zarno. Garth, we've got to do it, somehow. Once we find that power-source, we can use it! There'll be weapons the Ancients left, I'm sure of it. The murals at Chahnn showed they had weapons, strong enough to conquer the Zarno. If we can get those—"

"You're crazy," Garth said. "Plain crazy. What the hell do you expect me to do about it? Sampson would knock my block off if I tried to stop him now."

But he was thinking: *we're losing more than a chance to find the Ancient's power source. I'm losing my chance to find the cure for the Silver Plague.*

"No," he said stubbornly.

Paula's lip curled. "I should have known better than to ask you for help. I'll handle this myself." She unholstered her gun.

Garth looked at her. She'd fail. She couldn't handle these ten hard-shelled fighters, headed by Sampson. She'd fail. And, in the end, she'd go back to Earth, in the brig, back to the certain death of the Silver Plague. Oh, it might miss her, of course. But it might not.

Paula would die as Moira had done, years ago.

Garth shrugged and slapped the girl's weapon down. "Stay out of this," he commanded, and turned away, walking across the clearing to where Sampson and the others were shouldering their kits.

The red-haired giant looked up at Garth's approach. "Step it up," he said. "We're in a hurry."

"I'm not going."

Sampson's furry brows drew together. "The hell you're not. We need you!"

There was a band of ice around Garth's middle. "I know that. You can't get through without me. You'll never get out of the Forest alive. That's tough. Paula and I are going ahead, with Captain Brown. We're finishing what we started."

"You lousy so-and-so!" Sampson roared. His big hand reached out, clutching. Garth stepped back, drawing his pistol.

"Take it easy," he said under his breath. But there was a gun in Sampson's hand now. Behind the giant, the other men stirred angrily.

"You're coming with us!"

"Not alive. I won't be much good to you dead, will I?"

After a moment Sampson re-holstered his gun. He looked around at the others.

Someone said. "We can get along without that son."

Sampson growled at him. "Shut up. We can't. You'd have been sucked dry by that spider-thing yesterday if Garth hadn't seen it in time. He knows where to walk in this hell-hole."

Garth didn't say anything. He waited, holding his gun with casual lightness.

Sampson glared. "What do you want, then?"

"I want you to keep going—finish what you started."

"Then what?"

"We may find weapons—and other things."

"Suppose we don't?"

"Then we'll come back. I got you in here, and I'm the only man on Ganymede who can get you out."

Sampson's eyes narrowed. "Suppose we say yes. You can't keep a gun on us all the time. We might jump you. There are ways of making a man do things he doesn't want to do."

"Sure," Garth admitted, "you could torture me. Only that wouldn't help."

Sampson's gaze flicked past to the girl. Garth said quickly. "That wouldn't help either. Here's why. The antitoxin I gave you was too old. It isn't working the way it ought. Captain Brown was the first man to go under. But within three days, at the latest, every damn one of you will have Noctoli poison!"

Garth thought Sampson was going to shoot him then and there. A yell went up from the men.

Sampson's lifted hand quieted them. The giant was pale under his spaceburn.

"Is that straight?"

Garth nodded. "It's on the beam. Yeah. It'll take you a week to get out of the Forest, and you won't last that long, even if you force me to guide you. I don't think you can do that, anyway. But even if you did—within three days you'll be like the Captain. Walking dead men! You'll be okay at night, but you can't travel at night. By day you'll be living statues, sitting in the Forest waiting for the bloodsucker plants to come along and drain your blood, waiting for the poisonous butterflies to paralyze you and lay their eggs under your skin, waiting—you've seen what sort of things live in the Forest. Every day you'll be helpless. You can't run. Some night you'll wake up with your legs chewed off, or the butterfly maggots eating you alive. Like that? Well, that's what you'll get—and I'm the *only* guy that can save you!"

THE FACES of the men told Garth that his shots had gone home. The deadly menace of the forest, lurking always in the background, had worked into their nerves. Sampson's big hands clenched. "Damn you!" he snarled. "You can't—" Garth went on quickly. "I'm handing this to you straight. We're in a spot, sure, but we can get out of it. I can make more antitoxin, but it'll take a while. I can't do it while we're traveling. I need equipment. Here's what I'm proposing—we all keep going, the way we started. I'm immune to the pollen. If we move fast, we'll reach the lost city, or whatever it is, before you go under. Then I can start making antitoxin. We'll have to trap some small animals and allow time for incubation. But I'll be able to make fresh shots and neutralize the Noctoli pollen."

"It's too long a shot," Sampson said.

"Okay," Garth told him. "Suit yourself. Play it my way, or commit suicide." He turned and walked toward Paula, who had not moved from Brown's side.

Her eyes were steady on his. "Thanks. That was nice going—plenty nice, if you pull it off."

"It's suicide either way," Garth grunted. He began packing Brown's kit and his own.

Footsteps sounded. Garth didn't turn. He heard Sampson's deep voice, hoarse with repressed fear and rage.

"We're playing it your way, Garth. God help you if you make any boners!"

Sudden relief weakened Garth. He tried not to show it, though he realized that his hands were trembling.

"Fair enough," he said. "We'll march in ten minutes. Get the men ready."

Sampson muttered something and retreated. Garth slipped the pack on Brown's shoulders. The Captain, looking blankly ahead, didn't seem to notice.

"Keep your eye on him," Garth told Paula. "He'll be between us. He'll keep marching till we tell him to stop. See?"

She nodded, moistening her lips. "Y-yes. Is—that—going to happen to all of us?"

Garth said nothing. There wasn't anything to say.

But he knew, as he led the party away from the camp, how long a gamble he was undertaking. There were so many chances that he might fail! The odds were plenty tough—yet the stakes were equally high.

Had he known how difficult those odds were, Garth might not have risked it. For the Noctoli poison worked faster than he had guessed.

Meantime he guided ten sullen, fearful men, a walking corpse, and a girl deeper into the unexplored heart of the Black Forest. The Noctoli flowers breathed their poison from the underbrush, deadly and relentlessly.

CHAPTER SIX

THAT DAY they met a new enemy: jet-black lizards, five feet long, that clung to the black tree-boles, perfectly camouflaged, till the party came close. Then the reptiles flashed toward them, fanged jaws gaping. Constant alertness was all that saved them—that, and the blazing guns that killed the monsters.

Presence of the lizards was no respite from the other perils. The bloodsucker plants were more numerous, and the camouflage-moss made deceptively inviting paths through the red gloom. By dark, everyone was nearly exhausted, nerves worn to rags. Garth knew it would not take much for the men to explode into furious resentment against him.

Luckily, an hour after they had made camp. Captain Brown woke from his drugged trance, perfectly normal. But it took a while to make him understand what had happened.

For the first time Garth saw Brown lose his iron self-control, and then it was only for a moment. A flash of stark horror showed on the Captain's lean, hard face, to be gone instantly.

He lit a cigarette, his eyes brooding on Paula and Garth. Briefly he glanced past them to the men, preparing their rations.

"Uh-huh. Not so good. I suppose it's useless to think of traveling by night."

"It's impossible," Garth told him.

"You can make more antitoxin?"

"Sure—but not here. It's too dangerous. We've been safe so far because we've moved fast, camping at a different spot every night. If we holed up, we'd have a gang of monsters down on us in no time."

Brown considered. "It's a nasty business, having my own body go back on me. A bit of a shock. Well—" He let smoke drift from his nostrils. "Two more days ahead of us, eh? Then we reach the lost city."

"If it is a city. We don't even know that."

"But we do know there may be Zarno around. We'll have to arrive there soon after dark, so I'll be...conscious. If there's a fight, I want to be in on it. Why the devil didn't you test that antitoxin, Garth?" His voice was harshly angry.

Garth didn't answer. Brown had given him the rush act, but he wasn't making any excuses.

Paula said, "This isn't the best time to quarrel. You'd better talk to the men, Carver, so there'll be no trouble tomorrow."

"Yeah. Yeah, I suppose so."

Even the rebellious Sampson was convinced by Brown's well-chosen remarks.

They slept uneasily, with guards replaced every two hours, and the next day woke to find Captain Brown once more sunk into his Noctoli-trance. A few of the men complained of headaches.

By mid-morning Paula succumbed to the poison. Garth did not realize at first what had happened. Then, turning, he saw the girl's blank face and wide eyes fixed straight ahead as she marched along, and knew that she was entranced by the Noctoli till nightfall. The exercise of walking, speeding metabolism, had hastened the action of the virus.

They went on. An hour later another man went under. Then another. By noon only five men, including Garth and Sampson, were still conscious.

Their difficulties increased proportionately. They had to be on guard every second. The Noctoli victims walked quietly in line, but they did not react to danger. If the tentacles of a bloodsucker plant flashed out, they wouldn't try to escape. Their instinct of self-preservation had been dulled and blanketed.

The afternoon was pure hell. Garth, Sampson, and one other man had to guard and lead the rest. Their guns crashed incessantly, it seemed.

When they camped at the onset of darkness, Sampson and Garth alone remained.

THE red-haired giant, swaying on his feet, squinted at Garth, his face haggard with exhaustion.

"Nice going," he said sardonically, after a time. "What now? Maybe we'd better cut our throats."

Garth managed a shaky grin. "We're still okay. And there's only one more day left. Tomorrow—we'll make it then. We've got to."

Unwilling admiration showed in Sampson's eyes. "You're dead on your feet. I don't see how the hell you keep up this pace. Anyhow—we can't go back now. That's settled, anyway."

"Yeah. The others will wake up after a while. We'll have to stay on guard till then."

They did, guns drawn, peering at the silent depths of the Forest around them, while the rest of the party lay motionless, helpless against attack.

After a time Sampson spoke. Garth could not see his face in the heavy gloom. "What are you after, Garth?"

"Eh?"

"I had you ticketed wrong. A beachcomber... There must be something plenty important where we're going, or you wouldn't be so anxious to get there. What is it? Treasure, of course, but—jewels? Or what?"

Garth chuckled. "There may be. I don't know. Don't care."

"Hmmm..." Sampson was silent, baffled. Garth's mind swung back to that ever-present question. Had he killed Doc Willard? Very soon, now, he might know the answer.

But that was important only to him. The vital point was the black notebook Doc had had with him.

After a time Captain Brown stirred and sat up. Then the others. The men were a little panicky, but the presence of Brown and Sampson calmed them.

Garth, relieved of guard duty, had fallen asleep almost instantly.

He woke at dawn. Red twilight filtered down from above. The others were lying motionless in their blankets. Sampson's big body was huddled at the base of a tree.

Wearily Garth got up and went over to the giant. "Sampson!" he called. "Wake up! We've got a job—"

He stopped. Sampson's eyes were open, fixed and blank, and his dark cheeks had a significant ruddy flush.

The Noctoli poison—!

Garth stepped back, white to the lips. A sudden, horrible sense of loneliness pressed down on him. In the jungle things seemed to move, closing in menacingly.

He was alone now.

Alone—with twelve helpless companions to guard!

Somehow—somehow!—he had to get them through. One more day, and they would be at their goal. They could not stay here, that was certain.

Garth searched Sampson's pack till he found a half-empty whiskey bottle. He poured the burning stuff down his throat, though it rocked him back on his heels. But he needed artificial stimulation; it was the only thing that could keep him going now.

It helped. Garth took Sampson's gun and stuck it in his belt. If his own jammed or ran out of ammunition, today, it would be unfortunate.

One more day.

One more day!

Somehow, he got Sampson, Brown and the others lined up. They would march when he gave the word. The hypnotic trance of the Noctoli pollen had turned them into robots.

Garth put Paula directly behind him. The sight of her wan, drawn face made him feel a little frightened, though not for himself. He was remembering Moira, who had died on Earth years ago.

Eleven men and a girl—and he was the only one who could save them.

Garth made sure that the packs were in place on the men's shoulders. He took another drink, pulled out one of the guns, and gave the command to march.

Like automatons the line followed him.

If the day before had been hell, this was double-distilled hell.

Within an hour, Garth's nerves were scraped raw. He had to be constantly alert. The wrenching strain of watching for camouflaged menace made his eyes ache. When movement came, he had to be ready. Ready to squeeze the trigger…

He had to have eyes in the back of his head. For Sampson, at the tail of the procession, was as helpless as the others.

Liquor kept Garth going. Without it, he would have collapsed. By noon he was forced to call a halt, his eyes throbbing with the strain. But even then he could not relax. Danger waited everywhere.

He never remembered what happened that afternoon. He must have acted automatically, through blind instinct. But he got them through, somehow…

It was like awakening from deep sleep. Garth was abruptly conscious that he was marching forward, his head moving rhythmically, his eyes searching the jungle. The red twilight was almost gone.

He whirled, to see Paula directly behind him, unharmed. The others were strung out in single file—all of them, with Sampson's red head at the end. None was missing.

Garth shivered. His body was aching like fire. A quick glance showed him that his clothes were ribboned, his skin scratched raw, a long slash along his ribs. It had been treated with antiseptic, he saw, though he did not remember administering first aid, nor what had caused the wound.

What had wakened him? He peered through the gloom, making out a dark bulk, regular in outline, ahead and to his left. A few paces further gave him the answer. It was a building, of black stone or metal, no more than twelve feet high, and with an archway gaping in the nearest side.

Somehow it struck a chord of memory. They must be near their goal. No savages had built this structure. The Ancient Race?

The Zarno—they might be nearby. It would not do to encounter them now, while the men were in their Noctoli trance. And here, in the Forest, they were without cover—at the mercy of the Zarno should they appear.

Garth reconnoitered quietly, leading the others, for he dared not leave them alone. The black building seemed untenanted. He could vaguely make out a flight of steps leading down into darkness, and, more important than that, the threshold itself was thick with dust and mould. The—temple—was empty.

Which made it a good place to hide. Garth was beginning to realize he could not keep going much longer, at least without collapsing. But soon after dark the others would recover from their trance.

He stepped warily across the threshold, into the gloom of the temple. Simultaneously the flooring sank almost imperceptibly beneath his feet, and a deep, brazen bell-note boomed out, hushed with distance, as though it came from underground.

Indecision held Garth motionless for a moment. That clang was a signal of some sort—a warning against trespassers? A warning to *whom?*

HE WAS answered quickly. A low cry came, harsh and oddly familiar. It was the first of many. Garth, hesitating on the threshold, uncertain which way the danger lay, instinctively reached out his arm and dragged Paula close. She came obediently to his side, her eyes seeing nothing. The others—they stood like frozen statues.

Something flashed amid the underbrush. The scarlet tangle of vines and leaves was torn aside, and a figure leaped into view. A figure, man-like—yet not human!

At first glance it seemed to be a man in armor, more than six feet tall, and proportionately broad. Its body gleamed with reflected light. Neckless, its head was a hairless, shining ball whose only features were two oval, jet-black eyes. They were uncannily menacing.

A statue come to life! For the creature's body was obviously not flesh—it was hard, rough, and shiny as translucent glass. Silicate life!

Sprung from a silicon chemical base, as Earth life comes from carbon—but sentient, intelligent, and dangerous!

Others like it raced into view, pausing as they saw Garth and his companions. The first stepped forward. He had no mouth, but a circular diaphragm below and between his eyes vibrated rapidly, forming recognizable words.

"Al-khron ghanro ssel 'ri—"

It was the Ancient Tongue, which Garth had learned five years before and never forgotten. It came back to him easily now. He was beginning to remember other things, too. These creatures—he had seen them before. The Zarno—

"We come in peace." He raised one hand, his nerves jolting, waiting for the answer. Presently it came.

"You are not a god. The others with you are not gods. We are the Zarno; we destroy. We guard the house of the gods till they return."

Another of the silicate creatures pushed forward. "Do you not know this being, Kharn? Eight *ystods* ago he came here with another like him. Do you remember?"

Kharn nodded slowly. "That is true. We did not slay them then, for we thought they were messengers from the gods. They pretended to be—we were not sure. This one escaped. The other went into the Darkness."

The other? Doc Willard? Garth felt his throat tighten.

"The—Darkness? What is that?"

"The place from which only the gods return," Kharn said slowly.

Did he mean—death? Before Garth could ask, the second Zarno spoke.

"They must be taken and sacrificed, Kharn."

Garth took out his gun. "Wait," he said sharply, as the Zarno moved forward. "We have weapons. We can destroy you."

"You do not speak the truth. Only the gods can destroy us. Ages ago they came here and built their temple and taught us to be wise. When they left us, we stayed on, to guard the sacred places."

Garth's mouth felt dry. "We *are* messengers from the gods—" he declared.

"It is not true." Kharn began to walk forward. "Take them!"

Garth knew he had lost.

IT WAS like a nightmare, the steady, relentless approach of the monstrous beings. Garth held his gun leveled. His arm tightened around Paula's shoulders.

"Keep back," he commanded, conscious of the uselessness of the words.

Instead, Kharn and the others walked on. The creature's shining arm lifted, clamped on Garth's shoulder. He fired.

Kharn did not seem to feel the bullet, though it had not missed. Garth squeezed the trigger again. The pistol jolted against his palm.

The Zarno were—invulnerable!

Garth fought, nevertheless. He could see the silicate men lifting his companions like sacks of meal, hoisting them to gleaming shoulders, and carrying them, unresisting, through the forest. Paula was torn from his grasp. Cursing, he struck out at Kharn's impassive, inhuman face with the revolver-butt. Useless! Nothing could harm these creatures of living stone.

Ignoring his struggles, Kharn imprisoned Garth's arms and lifted him. Helpless, Garth was carried after the others. He forced himself to relax. A fury of impotent rage flooded him.

He battled it down. Better wait. A chance might come later; just now, there was none. Wait…

Through the forest they went on and on, a score of the silicate creatures, striding like armored giants in the darkening red glow. Not far. A pillar of black metal loomed before them soon, broken by an archway. Two of the monsters guarded it. For a moment Garth mistook the monolith for one of the ebony trees; then he realized his error as they crossed the threshold and began to descend a spiral ramp.

Now there was light, a cool, silvery radiance that seemed to come from the walls. Kharn's footsteps thumped hollow, tirelessly. Sudden weakness made Garth dizzy. He caught a glimpse of a well around which the ramp wound, a pit dropping away to the heart of a world, it seemed.

Utter exhaustion struck him like a physical blow.

CHAPTER SEVEN

HE REMEMBERED, dimly, what happened after that. It was like a series of fantastic visions, nightmare flashes of memory. At the bottom of the spiral was a cave, reminiscent of Chahnn and the other cities of the Ancients Garth had seen. Enigmatic machines loomed here and there. Unlike Chahnn, this city was lighted with the pale glow that came out of the walls and high-domed ceilings.

Cavern after cavern—peopled with the silicate creatures, filled with the dead machines of the Ancients! And, finally, an immense cave, its floor slanting up to a raised dais at one end. On the platform a throne of black metal stood, and seated upon it was a gigantic four-armed robot, larger than any Garth had ever seen before—standing, it would have been twelve feet tall, he judged.

Garth got only a glimpse of this. He was carried on swiftly to a smaller cavern where metal doors lined the walls. One of these was unlocked. He, with the other Earthmen, was carried within and dumped unceremoniously on the floor. The Zarno departed, clanging the door shut after them. Then—silence.

Garth staggered to his feet, staring around. The cell was oddly familiar. He had been in it, or one like it, five years ago with Doc Willard. The silvery light came from the waif, and there was a grating in the door. That was all.

He reached the grating and peered out. Two Zarno were on guard not far away. The lock—it might be possible to pick it, Garth thought, but the silicate creatures were invulnerable. So that would do no good.

Captain Brown's clipped voice said, "Where the hell are we, Garth?"

"Huh? Oh, you're awake." Garth laughed harshly. "You should have woken up half an hour ago. Not that it would have done any good—"

Brown stood up stiffly. "What d'you mean? What's happened?"

The others were waking now. For a few moments the cell was a babble of questions. One of the Zarno came briefly to the grill in the door and looked in. Shocked quiet greeted him.

After he had gone, Garth took advantage of the silence to say, "I'll tell you what's been going on, and then I'm going to sleep. I'll go to sleep anyway, unless I talk fast. I'm dead beat."

Sampson squinted at the door. "Tough customers. Shoot, Garth. I've got a hunch we're in a bad spot."

"We are. Listen—" Briefly Garth explained what had happened.

There were questions and counter-questions.

"You can speak their lingo, eh?"

"That won't help, Brown."

"They can't be invulnerable."

"They are—to our weapons. Silicate life!"

"When will they—sacrifice us?" Paula asked, a little shaken, though she tried not to show it.

Garth shrugged. "I don't know. Maybe I can talk 'em out of it. God knows. They worship the gods—the Ancients, I suppose—but they know we're not gods. So that's that."

"Well—"

THEY talked inconclusively. Sampson casually wandered over to the door, found a twisted scrap of wire, and used it on the lock. After a while he called softly to the others.

"This thing's a snap. It won't keep us in here."

Garth came over. "There are guards. It's no use."

One of the Zarno approached and peered in through the grill.

"Kharn has said you will not be hungry long. Tomorrow you will all die. You eat, like the creatures of the forest, do you not?"

"What's he saying?" Sampson muttered. "Nothing important." Garth switched to the Ancient Tongue. "It will be dangerous to kill us. We are messengers of the gods."

"We will believe that," the Zarno said, "when one of the gods tells us so." He nodded impassively and retreated.

Paula touched Garth's arm. "Isn't there any way—"

"I don't know. Maybe. Maybe not."

"There's light here. There's none in the other cities of the Ancients. That means the power-source still works here. If we can find it—"

Garth couldn't look at her, knowing they were doomed to die the next day. He shrugged, turned away, and found an empty corner. Ignoring the others, he tried to relax on the hard floor. His brain just wasn't working now. It was fagged out. He had a vague hunch that there might be a way out—but he was too exhausted to follow it up now. A few hours' sleep was vital.

But he slept past dawn. When he awoke, he saw the others lying motionless, their eyes fixed in the blank stare of the Noctoli trance.

Glancing at the chronometer on Brown's wrist, Garth figured swiftly. It was past dawn. That meant there was little time left in which to act—provided action was possible. But sleep had refreshed him, though his muscles still ached painfully. He was beginning to remember what his hunch had been.

When he and Doc Willard had been captives, there had been guards only at night. During the long Ganymedean day, none was necessary, for the Noctoli poison had been active then. By day, the Zarno thought, men of flesh were tranced and helpless. Unless...

Garth moved quietly to the door. Through the grill he saw the cave, empty of life. There were no guards. He was glad he had slept past dawn, so that the Zarno were able to believe him entranced like the others.

But what now? Escape? To where? There was still power in the lost city; perhaps the weapons of the Ancients still existed. Weapons stronger than guns to conquer the Zarno! But, regardless of that, it was necessary to find a hiding-place. This was the day of sacrifice.

Ironic thought—a hiding-place in an underground city teeming with the Zarno!

Garth shrugged. The door was locked, he discovered, and it took time to find the twisted wire Sampson had used. Even then, Garth was unable to manipulate the intricate tumblers. He scowled, chewing his lip, and eying the wire. Sampson's skilled fingers were necessary.

He roused the red-haired giant and led him to the door. Sampson looked straight ahead, his eyes dull. He obeyed when Garth spoke—but that was all. Was his skill sufficiently instinctive to be used now?

There was only one way to find out. Garth put the wire in Sampson's hand. "Unlock the door."

He had to repeat the command twice before Sampson understood. Then the big man bent, fumbling with the lock, working with agonizing slowness.

Hours seemed to drag past before Sampson straightened.

GARTH tried the door. It opened. The first step was accomplished, anyhow. The others would be more difficult. He was unfamiliar with the underground city. How the devil could he evade the Zarno and find a hiding-place? Alone, he would have a better chance. But he had twelve companions to take with him.

He spoke to each of them. "Follow me. You understand? Follow me till I tell you to stop. Move as quietly as you can."

Then he led them out of the cell.

The city, as he speedily learned, was a labyrinth. Luckily there were innumerable cross-passages. And all the cities of the Ancients had been built along a similar plan. Garth knew the layout of Chahnn, and that helped him now. But there were times when he had to move fast, and the others walked as though striding through water.

"Quick! In here! *Fast!*"

And they would follow him, into a side tunnel, while the heavy, metallic footsteps of the Zarno approached like the drums of doom.

But there was no place to hide permanently. Worst of all, a distant clanging sounded presently, and Garth guessed what that meant. The escape of the captives had been discovered.

Gingerly he skirted the huge cave where the dais was, glimpsing the giant robot in the distance, and shepherding his charges along a twisting corridor that led down. But the footsteps were growing louder. Garth was almost certain that they were following.

He increased his pace, with wary glances behind him. Unless he found a side passage soon, the swift Zarno would speedily overtake them.

"Faster! Move faster!"

The Earthmen tried to obey. Like automatons they ran, their eyes fixed and staring, while the clamor of pursuit grew louder. Looking back. Garth saw a flash of shining movement. The Zarno!

"Faster!"

There were no side tunnels. They came out into a small cave, completely empty. It was a cul-de-sac. Light was reflected brightly from three walls.

The fourth wall was dead black—neither rock nor stone. It was like a jet curtain, blocking their path. Garth jerked to a halt, knowing the utter hopelessness of futility. They were trapped now.

The Zarno were pursuing, unmistakably.

Garth took out his useless gun. His face was set in grim lines. What good were bullets against the silicate creatures?

But waiting helplessly was far worse. At least he could try to fight.

He had forgotten to command his charges to halt. Glancing around, Garth saw something that made his eyes widen in incredulous amazement. Paula was walking toward the black curtain…the wall…

She stepped through it and vanished.

Brown followed her. Then another man. And another.

Last of all, Sampson, disappearing like a ghost through the blackness!

Heavy footsteps whirled Garth about. Down the corridor he could see the flashing gleams that heralded the Zarno. His tight grin was a grimace.

"The hell with your pals," he said softly—and turned again. He raced in pursuit of the others.

Leaped through the dark curtain!

THERE was an instant of grinding, jolting shock that left him blind. He staggered, caught himself, and saw that he was in a passage that led toward a distant brightness. Silhouetted against the glow were the moving figures of his companions.

He sprinted after them. But he did not overtake them till they had emerged in a cavern unlike any he had seen before. "Okay! Stop! Stop, that's right." They halted, motionless.

Garth looked behind him, but there was no trace of the Zarno.

This cavern was lighted like the others. But there were fewer machines. Row after row of the giant four-armed robots stood like an army on the dark-metal floor. The walls were jeweled, thousands of pearly disks studding them. A low humming came from a machine nearby, a tripod with lenses surmounting a square box.

Garth walked through it He hesitated, glanced around again, and then peered through the lenses.

A voice seemed to speak within his brain.

"—invoked the rule of silence. After that, Genjaro Lo declared that space travel was inevitable and might solve the natural problems of our civilization—"

It had spoken in the Ancient Tongue. And, at the same time. Garth had seen a picture of a huge, four-armed being with a bulging, yet oddly symmetrical head, standing on a rostrum addressing a multitude…

"Ed!" The voice rang through the silent cavern. "Ed Garth! You made it!"

Garth whirled. A man had emerged from a cavern-mouth nearby, a short, slight man with white hair and a lined, tired face. He ran forward, his ragged garments flapping, his eyes shining.

Garth said, in a voice like a prayer, "Doc Willard. *You're alive!*"

CHAPTER EIGHT

WILLARD gripped his friend's hands.

"Alive, yes. If you can call it that. I've been living for only one thing. I knew you'd come back, with help, if you got through. And you did!"

The cavern was spinning around Garth. He braced himself, staring at the man.

"Doc! I've been going crazy for five years. I thought I—I'd killed you."

Willard stared. "Killed me? But—"

"That altar!" The words tumbled out of Garth's mouth. "I couldn't remember much. That damned Noctoli poison—I lost my memory. But I knew I'd tried to knife you while you were stretched out on an altar—"

Sympathy showed in Willard's eyes. "Good Lord, Ed! And you could remember only that? You must have gone through hell."

"I did. I didn't know what—"

"But we planned it. The whole thing. A fake ceremony, to impress the Zarno and give us a chance to escape. They thought we *might* be messengers from their gods—the Ancients—and we told 'em so, after we'd learned their language. The sacrifice—it was a fake, that's all. And it went through as we planned. You pretended to stab me, and while the Zarno were bowing and genuflecting, we got away. At least you did. They recaptured me.

Garth shook his head. "Tell me. I don't know, really."

Willard glanced at the Earthmen, curiosity in his eyes. "You've a bit of explaining to do yourself, Ed. Are they—Noctoli?"

"Yeah. I worked out an antitoxin, but it was stale." Quickly Garth explained what had happened.

"I see. Well—got a cigarette?" Willard sucked the smoke luxuriously into his lungs. "That's good. Five years since I had one of these. Sit down and let's talk. No chairs, but try the floor."

"Okay. What happened to you?"

"Nothing much. When we staged our fake ceremony—the Zarno are plenty religious—I headed for that little black temple in the forest. Know the place?"

"Yeah. That's where they caught us."

"Well, it leads to freedom. There's an underground tunnel that takes you out in a camouflaged hangar. The Ancients had antigravity. I found out later, and their flying-boats were hidden there. They're still good, Ed. They still work. I'd have got away if the Zarno hadn't been right on my heels."

"So?"

Willard nodded. "The controls are easy. A couple of push buttons and a steering lever. I'd got a few feet off the ground when a couple of Zarno jumped into the boat with me. They heaved me out and followed. The flying-boat went off to Mars or somewhere, I suppose—it kept on going straight up. But there are others. Only I've never been able to get at them. If I could have, I'd have headed for Oretown, pronto."

Garth's eyes were glowing. "If we could reach that hangar, Doc, we could escape—all of us."

"Sure. Only we can't. Too many guards. It's impossible to get out of this city. I've tried often enough. The only way I managed to survive was by entering the Darkness." His voice trailed away.

"That black wall?"

"It's a vibration-barrier. None of the Zarno can pass it. It shakes them to pieces—destroys them. The Ancients made it, I suppose, to guard their library." Willard extended his hand in a sweeping gesture. "This is it. All the knowledge of the Ancients—tremendous knowledge—compiled here for reference. If we could only get it out to the world!"

Garth remembered something. "Does it mention their power-source?"

"Sure. I've had nothing to do for five years but study the library. I could put my finger on the wire-tape recording that explains the process. It's an intricate business, but we could duplicate it on Earth easily enough."

Paula would be glad to know that, Garth thought. The secret of the Ancients' power, that could replace oil and coal—a vital secret to Earth now.

WILLARD was still talking. "I ran when I heard you coming. I'd been studying one of the recordings, but I thought the Zarno might have got through the barrier somehow... It doesn't harm humans, luckily, or the robots. I learned a lot in five years."

"How did you manage to keep alive?"

"I found food. The Ancients had stocked up this place. *Pills!*" Willard grimaced. "They kept me alive, and there was a machine for making water out of the air. But I'm hungry for a steak."

Garth scowled. "Doc—one more thing. You know what I mean?"

Willard sobered. "I get it, Ed. The cure. Whether or not I—"

"Whether or not you've found the cure for the Silver Plague. It hasn't been checked yet. It's still killing thousands on Earth."

"So. I wondered a lot about that. Well—the answer is yes, Ed. I know the answer."

"The cure?"

"Yes. I worked it out, completely, with the aid of the Ancients' library. They were studying it too, but they didn't have quite the right angle. However, they were able to supply the missing data I needed." Willard took from his pocket a small notebook. "I had five years to work on it. So far, of course, it's theoretical, but everything checks. It's the cure, all right."

Somehow Garth didn't feel much excitement. Five years ago, he thought, that notebook would have saved Moira's life. Now—well, it would still save life. It would save Earth. But—

He shrugged. "Two good reasons to get back to civilization. The cure, and the secret of the power-source."

Willard nodded. "The Ancients died of the Silver Plague, indirectly. They tried to escape by changing their bodies. The library told me that."

"Their bodies? How?"

"Well—you've seen the robots in Chahnn and here. Originally they were the servants of the Ancients."

"Intelligent?"

"No—not in the way you mean. They could be conditioned to perform certain tasks, but usually they were controlled telepathically by the Ancients, who wore specialized helmet-transmitters for the purpose. The robots had radio-atomic brains that reacted to telepathic commands. Then when the Silver Plague struck, the Ancients tried to escape by transplanting, not their physical brains, but their *minds*. I don't quite know how it was done. But the thought-patterns, the individual mental matrix of each Ancient were somehow impressed on the radio-atomic brain of a robot. Their minds were put into the robots' brains—and controlled the metal bodies. So they escaped the Plague. But they died anyway. Human, intelligent minds can't be transplanted successfully into artificial bodies that way. So—in a hundred years—they were dead, all of them."

So that was the secret of the Ancients' disappearance from Ganymede. They had taken new bodies—and those bodies had killed them through their sheer alienage.

Willard crushed out his cigarette-stub. "All the knowledge of the Ancients at my finger-tips, Ed. You can imagine what research I've done!"

"I should have thought you'd have looked for a weapon against the Zarno," Garth said practically. "The Ancients were able to conquer them."

"I did—first of all, after I'd learned how to work the recording-machines. A certain ray will destroy them—a vibrationary beam that shakes them to pieces, disrupts their molecular structure. The only trouble is—" Willard grinned sardonically. "It takes a damn good machine shop to build such a projector."

"Oh. We couldn't—"

"We couldn't. The Ancients left plenty of apparatus here, but not the right kind. Mostly records, and a lot of robots. Sorry, Ed, but unless you brought good weapons with you, you're stuck here with me."

GARTH looked around to where his companions were standing motionless. "Yeah. Looks like it. Unless we can break through to that hangar of antigravity ships—"

"We can't. The city's full of the Zarno, day and night. And there are always guards outside."

Garth sighed. "The trouble is, unless we get out, nothing can stop the Silver Plague. Not to mention the fuel shortage. Wait a minute. You said the Zarno were superstitious—we tricked them once with a fake ceremony. Couldn't we try that again?"

"I did," Willard told them. "It didn't work. The Zarno know what human beings are like now. Only the gods would impress them—those robots who once were their masters."

Garth stopped breathing for a moment. "There's a way," he said.

Willard looked at him. "I don't think so. When I saw you'd come back, I hoped for a minute—but it's no use. The Zarno are invulnerable to any weapons we can create here. We can't get out of the city!"

"You said the gods would impress them."

"The gods are dead—the Ancients."

"Suppose one of them came back?" Willard caught his breath. "What do you mean?"

"Originally the robots were controlled telepathically. Why can't that work now—for us?"

"Don't you imagine I thought of that? But it's no use, without one of them helmet-transmitters. And there aren't any…" Willard sucked in his breath. "Hold on! I'd forgotten something. There's one transmitter left—just one. But it's not a portable."

"Swell!"

"Wait a minute. Come over here." The older man led the way to a tripod-projector, found a cylindrical black object, and slipped it into place. "Look at this."

Peering through the eyepieces, Garth recognized the great cavern with the dais at one end. The scene shifted, showing the gigantic twelve-foot robot sitting on its throne, a solid block of black metal.

"Watch," Willard said.

A voice spoke in Garth's mind, in the Ancient Tongue. "It was necessary to impress the superstitious Zarno. Thus we created this robot god and placed it on its throne. Its radio-atomic brain can be controlled telepathically by means of a transmitter concealed within the throne."

The scene changed, showing the back of the ebony block. A hand, inhuman and six-fingered, came into view—the hand of an Ancient. It touched a concealed spring, and the throne's back slid open, revealing a compartment easily large enough to hold a man.

"Here is the transmitter. It is placed on the head and the will focused on issuing telepathic commands to the robot god on the throne."

There was more, but now Garth watched with only half his mind. He scarcely saw the details of the ritual ceremony with which the Ancients had impressed the Zarno. When the vision vanished, he swung about, a new light in his eyes.

"That's it, Doc! That robot god's going to come to life!"

WILLARD FROWNED. *"Ummm…* The gadget isn't difficult to operate—I've learned that much from the recordings. You just think hard, that's all. But—"

"The god will come to life and summon the Zarno—all of them. The rest of you can escape while I'm keeping 'em busy."

"Hold on!" the doctor snapped. "Why you? It's my job, if it's anybody's."

"Sorry," Garth said. "It doesn't work out that way. You're the only guy who can cure the Silver Plague. Unless you get out safely, it's the end of Earth."

Willard didn't answer. Garth went on swiftly.

"You could reach the hangar if it weren't for the Zarno. Well, I'll get inside that throne and start the ruckus. That'll give you time." His voice was emotionless.

"How do you know you could reach that temple-cave? The city's full of Zarno."

Garth shrugged. "It's a chance we've got to take. The only one."

Willard chewed his lip. "Why the devil do you have to be the one?"

"Because I know the Ancient Tongue. The robot can talk, can't it? Well! It's between you and me, Doc, and you're the boy who can cure the Silver Plague. You can't get away from that."

"I—I suppose so. But—"

"You know the way out. Give me time to reach the temple and begin the ceremony. Then lead the others out. They'll obey you; they're in the Noctoli trance. Get 'em to the hangar and light out for Oretown. Be sure to take the recording of the power-source with you."

"You crazy fool," Willard said through stiff lips. "What about Moira?"

Garth's face went gray. "Moira died years ago," he said carefully. "It was the Silver Plague."

Doc didn't reply. But he nodded as though he had unexpectedly learned the answer to a problem that had been puzzling him.

"Okay," Garth said. "You know what to do. Give me time enough to make it. Then get out of here with the others, fast."

Willard's hand gripped Garth's. "Ed—"

"Forget it."

He moved toward the tunnel-mouth. Paula, he saw, was lying nearby, her red-gold hair cascading about her pale, lovely face.

Garth stood looking down at her for a long moment. Then he went on, into the tunnel that waited for him. He did not look back.

Cautiously he stepped through the black curtain, ready to retreat at sight of any Zarno. But the cavern was empty.

If he could make it—!

Noiselessly he stole up the passage. Once he froze against the wall at the sound of distant footsteps. But they faded and were gone.

He came out at last into a corridor he recognized. Far away, he saw the flashing gleam of the Zarno's silicate skins. They were approaching, but apparently had not seen him yet.

He raced for the archway that led into the temple-cavern. If there were any Zarno there, it would be fatal. But luck favored him. The immense room was empty. At the far end the huge robot sat on its jet throne.

Garth sprinted across the floor. He could hear voices growing louder in the distance, and the thumping of the Zarnos' footsteps, but he dared not risk a glance behind. Could he make it?

He jerked to a halt, springing behind the throne, its bulk temporarily hiding him. The Zarno were in the temple-cave now; he could tell that by their voices. Hastily he sought the secret spring.

A panel opened in the ebon block. It was exactly as he had seen it on the tripod-recording machine, a fair-sized cubicle with light coming faintly through a vision-slit in one wall. Garth wedged himself in and slid the panel shut behind him, gasping with relief. Peering through the slit, he found he could see the entire cavern. Three Zarno were approaching.

The robot, seated on the throne above him, was, of course, invisible. Garth stared around, trying to remember the details of the Ancients' recording. A helmet transmitter...there it was, attached by wires to the low ceiling. Warily Garth slipped it upon his head.

What now?

A flat black plate, like a diaphragm, was set in the wall slightly above his head as he crouched. This hiding-place, he realized, had been built for the larger bodies of the Ancients.

Closing his eyes, he tried to concentrate. Doc Willard had said that the helmet transmitters worked that way. Telepathy…will power…

"Stand up!" he commanded silently to the unseen robot above him. "Stand up!"

There was a stir of movement. Garth, peering through the slit, saw the three Zarno jerk to a halt.

One of them cried, "The gods return! *Kra-enlarnov! The gods!"*

GARTH put his mouth close to the diaphragm. His words, amplified, rolled out through the cavern in the Ancient Tongue.

"Yes—the gods return! Summon the Zarno! Let none fail to obey the summons!"

Shouts went up. The Zarno whirled and raced away. For the moment, Garth was alone.

He concentrated on the transmitter again, commanding the robot to move forward to the edge of the dais, till he could see its back.

"Raise your arm. Step back. Forward again. Back."

It worked. The robot obeyed his mental commands, awkwardly, but—it obeyed.

"Back. Sit on the throne."

A jarring crash deafened Garth momentarily. He had forgotten how huge the robot was. No doubt the creature should lever itself down gradually into its seat, instead of dropping a ton of metal solidly on the black block.

Footsteps again. The Zarno were beginning to pour into the cavern. Huge as it was, they almost filled it. They flung themselves flat, crawling toward the dais, nodding their misshapen heads in awkward rhythm. Their voices were raised in a deep-throated chant.

Garth concentrated. At his mental command, the robot rose and paced slowly forward.

"Kra-enlar!"

Garth put his mouth to the diaphragm. His voice crashed out.

"The gods have returned! Hear me, O Zarno!"

"We hear!"

"Let no Zarno fail to come to the temple of the gods. Have the guards left their posts?"

"Nay—nay!"

"Summon them," Garth roared. "When the gods speak, all must hearken. Let every Zarno come to me now, or die!"

Some of the creatures raced away and returned with others. The chant continued.

"Have any Zarno failed to heed my summons?"

"None—none! We are here—all!"

Garth nearly shouted with relief. There were almost two thousand Zarno in the cavern, he judged, all genuflecting before the dais. And that meant that the city was unguarded—that Doc Willard could lead the others to the anti-gravity hangar.

If he could hold the Zarno here!

Garth shook his head, feeling oddly dizzy. He tried to concentrate. At his mental order, the giant robot lifted its arms in symbolic, ritualistic gestures he remembered from the tripod-recorder.

But the dizziness persisted. Garth realized that his lungs were hurting. He found it difficult to draw a deep breath.

Air—he needed fresh air! The inhuman lungs of the Ancients probably were able to endure lack of oxygen far better than the human organism. In any case—Garth realized that the air was getting stale.

He investigated the vision-slit. It was barred by a glassy, transparent pane that seemed as hard as steel. Well, it would be necessary to open the panel behind him—a few inches, anyway. Garth's hand sought for the spring. It was in plain sight; there was no need to conceal it within the throne's compartment.

He pressed it. There was a low grinding that stopped almost immediately. Garth tried again.

Useless. The mechanism, somehow, was jammed. Probably its mechanism had failed when the huge robot had crashed down on the throne.

That meant…

Garth's fingers tried to find some purchase on the smooth surface of the panel. He failed…

A Zarno called a question. Garth turned back to the eye-slit, trying to fight back his dizziness. Heads were lifted, he saw, watching him inquiringly, as though the silicate creatures expected something. Well…

He made the robot move again, its arms reaching out in ancient ceremonial gestures. A gasp of awe came from the Zarno.

Their chant thundered out, deeper, sonorous, and inhuman.

GARTH felt the beginning of a throbbing ache in his temples. He was trapped here. How long could he stand it? He was human, not one of the Ancients. He needed air—

He held the Zarno, but not for long. Once more bulbous heads were lifted, oval eyes watching him inquiringly. They were expecting something—what? Garth tried to remember what he had seen in the recorder.

More heads were lifted.

Garth made the robot step forward, raising its metal arms. He had to say something—anything that would hold the Zarno quiet for a while, long enough for Doc and the others to escape. Words he had forgotten since childhood came suddenly, unexpectedly to him. The English phrases meant nothing to the Zarno, but the sonorous, powerful chant kept them silent.

"He shall deliver thee from the snare of the hunter; and from the noisome pestilence… Thou shalt not be afraid for any terror by night; nor for the arrow that flieth by day… A thousand shall fall beside thee, and ten thousand at thy right hand; but it shall not come nigh thee."

The agony flamed up again in Garth's brain, consuming, terrible. The huge robot body of the dais swayed, caught itself, and the chant thundered out again through the great cavern.

"If I take the wings of the morning; and remain in the uttermost parts of the sea; even there also shall thy hand lead me…

The distant, harsh clangor of a bell sounded. Garth had heard it before, when he had crossed the threshold of the black temple in the forest. At the sound the Zarno stirred, and a few of them sprang up.

Garth thrust out his hand, fighting back the pain that tore at him like white flame.

His voice held them…

"The floods are risen, O Lord, the floods have lifted up their voices; the floods lift up their waves… The waves of the sea are mighty, and rage horribly, but yet the Lord, who dwelleth on high, is mightier—"

He held them. He held them, speaking a tongue they did not know, while his mind shook under the impact of sanity-destroying pain. A slow, sick bitterness crept into his soul. Was this the end—death here, imprisoned on an alien world, so far from his home planet?

Death—and for what?

He closed his mind to the thought. Mentally he paced Doc and the others through the tunnel, from the black temple to the hangar. Surely they must have reached it by now! Paula—

That first glimpse he had had of the girl, in Tolomo's drinking-hell—Moira, he had thought then, for an incredible instant. Yes, she had been like Moira. If the paths of destiny had led elsewhere than to the Black Forest of Ganymede, the result might have been far distant. He would not be dying here alone, horribly alone. Moira—Paula—

They were the same, somehow. And Garth knew he had to keep going, till he had saved Paula Trent. A little time—a few moments more, to keep the Zarno in check.

He and Moira had been cheated of their lives, their futures in some way he could not quite understand. But there remained Paula. She must not die. She and the others must get through.

"Ed."

Garth's heart answered that soundless call. His lips formed the name *Moira.*

SHE was there, beside him, and he did not question, did not even wonder. It was enough that she had come back. Her brown ringlets curled about the pale face as he remembered, and the blue eyes held love and—something more.

A message.

"What is it, Moira? What—" He reached out hungry arms.

"Ed. It isn't only us. It's Earth. Don't stop now, Ed. A few more minutes to hold the Zarno back; that will be enough. Be strong. A little time more—such a little time, and then you can rest."

A phantom born of his delirium. Garth knew, but she was no less real for that. He tried to speak and failed. His chest constricted with pain. Outside the altar, the Zarno were stirring uneasily.

"I—I can't—"

"You must."

Anger swept through him. "Why? We've been cheated of everything, Moira! Our heritage—"

She smiled at him, very tenderly. "The grass is still green on the hills of Earth, my lover. Have you forgotten? The little streams that go laughing down the valleys, and the ocean surging up to the white beaches? There are still sunsets on Earth, and men and women will see them for ages to come. Men who might have been our sons; women who might have been our daughters. And they are our children, Ed, as surely as though we had given them birth. For we are giving them life. There will be a future for mankind because of us. We have given up our own lives that our children may live, and go on to glories we can never know ourselves. It is Earth that needs your help now—and that is something greater than either of us."

Something greater…

The Zarno were beginning to move forward, and some of them were sidling toward the passage. Garth, gasping for breath, summoned all his reserve energy. He seemed to feel Moira's cool hand on his shoulder, silently urging him on.

Something greater…

"The days of man are but as grass," he croaked, and the amplified sound went thundering through the temple, halting the Zarno where they stood. They turned again to the altar.

"For he flourisheth as a flower of the field…for as soon as the wind goeth over, it is gone—"

He held them, somehow, knowing that Moira stood beside him. Toward the end, Garth was no longer conscious of his surroundings. The Zarno swam before his eyes, changing, altering, and abruptly they vanished. In their place was…was…

He saw Earth, as he remembered it, the loveliest planet of all. He saw the heartbreaking beauty of flaming sunsets over the emerald seas, and the snowy purity of high peaks lifting above baking deserts. He felt the cold blast of Earthwinds on his cheeks, the stinging, exciting chill of mountain streams against his skin. There was the warm smell of hay, golden in the fields; the sharpness of eucalyptus and pine; the breath of the little bright flowers that grow only on Earth.

He heard the voices of Earth. The chuckling of brooks, and the deep shouting of the gale; the lowing of cattle, the sound of leaves rustling, and the crash of angry breakers. The soul of Earth spoke to the man who would never see it again.

He listened, while he chanted the majestic, rolling syllables that kept the Zarno in check. Beside him was Moira. Beneath him, his own world, green and beautiful.

And across the emerald planet men and women came marching, the sunlight making a golden path for them as they moved out of darkness into the unknown brightness of the future. They were like gods, great-limbed, lovely, and with eyes fearless as a falcon's filled with laughter.

Before their marching feet the road of the ages unrolled. Mighty cities reared to the blue skies of Earth, and ships swept out beyond the stars, binding the galaxies and the universe with unbreakable chains of life. Outward and ever outward the circles of humanity and civilization rippled.

Men and women like gods, unafraid, knowing a life greater than ever before…

And they turned questioning eyes on Garth, asking him the question on which their existence depended.

"Will you save us? Will you give us life? Will you give us the future you yourself can never know?"

Garth answered them in his own way, with Moira beside him. For now it did not matter that he was dying; he had found something greater than he had ever known before.

Through the temple his voice rang like brazen trumpets.

"—the wind bloweth...and the place thereof shall know it no more."

A PANEL in the wall by his head lit up, making a square of brightness. He strained his eyes at it, discerning a picture. A scanner of some sort. It showed a transparent ovoid slanting up through the black trees of the forest, a ship with Doc Willard at the controls and eleven men and a girl in the vessel with him—a girl with red-gold hair, going back to Earth, with the knowledge that would save a world from destruction.

He had not failed.

The picture on the scanner darkened. The burning ache in Garth's lungs grew worse. If he could breathe—

On the dais, the robot swayed, its metal legs giving beneath its weight. The crash of its fall brought the Zarno to their feet, frozen with amazement for a moment. Then they moved forward like a wave.

Garth saw them, dimly, through the vision-slit. A white curtain of pain blotted them out. He was dying; he knew that. The shouts of the Zarno came to him faintly.

"...the wind bloweth...and the place thereof shall know it no more..."

But in that place the seeds of the future would grow. Once more Garth saw the children of Earth's unborn generations, and this time the question in their eyes was answered. They would live and go on, to the stars, and beyond.

Moira was beside him. Her cool hand touched his; she came into his arms.

And the white curtain flamed agonizingly for the last time.

Then, mercifully, there was no more pain. Under the black throne Garth's body lay motionless in its strange tomb.

The Zarnos' cries filled the temple as they mourned their dead god—but the man who had saved Earth did not hear them.

THE END

Made in the USA
Middletown, DE
29 June 2021